THE MONTC...

Their eyes met . . . and a legend began

It was at the French court that renegade Charles de Montclair first kissed the hand of the beautiful Angélique . . . and lost his heart. Angélique, too, was bewitched. Though promised in marriage to a powerful duke, she defied the dictates of society and eloped with her lover.

On his secluded estate they began a lifetime of bliss. And as a symbol of his devotion, Charles gave his bride an exquisite set of jewelry—the four matchless Montclair emeralds. Angélique cherished the gift, knowing her husband's love shone from each glittering stone.

A century later revolution rocked France, and this noble couple's great-great-granddaughter was forced to flee for her life. Snatching up a few possessions in the dead of night, she made her tortuous way to freedom in the New World. Much as she treasured her family's gift of love, she was forced to sell the precious jewels, one by one. And each carried with it the legacy of the past into the future. . . .

Cofounder and first president of the Romance Writers of America, **Rita Clay Estrada** didn't start out to be a writer. She studied art and psychology, worked as a model, a secretary, a salesperson and a bookstore manager. Along the way, she also settled in Texas, married and raised four children. Then she read her first Harlequin and found her true calling. Today she has a large and loyal following, as witnessed by the immense popularity of her six Temptations. In 1988 she also won an *Affaire de Coeur* Silver Pen Certificate.

Books by Rita Clay Estrada

HARLEQUIN TEMPTATION

Trust

RITA CLAY ESTRADA

Harlequin Books

TORONTO • NEW YORK • LONDON
AMSTERDAM • PARIS • SYDNEY • HAMBURG
STOCKHOLM • ATHENS • TOKYO • MILAN

Published September 1988

ISBN 0-373-25320-6

1

CLAY REYNOLDS strode into the Hilton Ballroom to assure himself that everything was in readiness for that night. Once a year he gave a cocktail party, mainly to thank his associates for their business, although a few close friends would be there as well. He wasn't fond of occasions that pressured him into inane congeniality, nor was he fond of crowds, but socializing was good for business so he had no choice.

Tonight he felt even more pressured than usual. Tonight the woman he'd decided to marry was going to play hostess. He wanted everything to be perfect. He wanted *her* to be perfect, to reinforce his occasionally shaky decision to marry her.

On the champagne table stood a fountain and glasses, and centered on the hors d'oeuvres table was a large ice sculpture of a playful dolphin. On either side of the room was a bar, each bartender busily stocking it with ice and drinks. The polished dance floor was surrounded by tables covered in spotless white tablecloths. There was an area set aside for a three-piece combo, so the musicians would be screened off from the general hubbub.

Everything was perfect. He nodded approval to one of the men assisting at the hors d'oeuvres table, then turned and walked back down the hall to the elevator. After eight years the annual party was a tradition, and so was his rented suite. He figured if he had to arrive early and be the last one to leave, he might as well stay the night. It worked out very well.

As he entered his suite the telephone was ringing.

"Yes?" He spoke absently while weighing the decision to either change into his tuxedo or have a drink first.

"Hello, darling. I just wanted to hear your voice." Magda's deliberately low-pitched tone filtered over the phone. Though phony, it was also very effective.

"Are you ready for this evening?" He pulled at the knot of his tie, then loosened the top button of his shirt.

"I can't wait. I hope you like my dress. It's just a tiny bit daring."

"As long as no one touches you but me," he answered almost by rote. There were certain things he had learned to say to keep his dates happy. Possessiveness seemed to be a sign they cherished. Sexual arousal was another. He had to remind himself that Magda wasn't just another date—she was his bride-to-be.

"Oh," she chuckled low, "you mean you'd fight for me, darling?" Her voice promised what the reward to him would be for a black eye.

He smiled cynically. "Of course. I just can't guarantee I'll win."

"With your broad shoulders and strong arms?" Her voice was a sexy whisper that irritated him rather than leaving him wanting more. "Besides you never lose at anything."

"There's always a first time, Magda." He shrugged out of his coat and flung it on the bed, impatient now to take a shower, pour a drink and relax before donning his best smile and manners. "The car will pick you up at eight. Right now, I'm headed for the shower, so I'll see you then." It was a statement and a closing.

The line sang with silence for a few seconds, and Clay could almost feel Magda's disappointment that he wouldn't play the game anymore. "I'll see you then, darling," she promised, apparently having recovered quickly.

"I'll be waiting for you." He hung up without even saying goodbye. Suddenly he felt tired.

Sinking to the edge of the bed, he held his head in his hands. A vision of Magda danced in front of his eyes. She was classically beautiful, with bone structure that most models would be envious of. She was slim but well formed in all the right places. Her sense of color and design was impeccable. So why the sudden doubt?

It was ridiculous! Forcing any thoughts away that didn't fit his original plans, he undid his cuffs, shrugged out of his shirt and threw it across the bottom of the bed. He was marrying to have a home and children and a gracious hostess, and he had selected his prospective wife with that specific purpose in mind. The decision concerning who would share his private life and income was just as important as any big business deal, and it deserved as much deliberation as everything else he had done to build himself into a success. There was nothing haphazard about his choice or his requirements in a wife. It would work.

He ignored the niggling doubt in the back of his mind. Magda and Clay had tentatively discussed a premarital contract just last night and he knew she would sign. It would ensure both of them a measure of security. It was that simple. Contracts were a way of life with him, and without them he felt vulnerable.

It was a shame his parents hadn't signed one, but with their outlook, they wouldn't have kept the terms anyway. But they *had* taught him one hell of a lesson: never trust anyone—not even parents—not to aim for the jugular. His parents were certainly past masters at it. They always said they'd fallen in love at first sight, but Clay knew that everything after that had been a fight. His own observation was that most parents left a lot to be desired when it came to raising a child in a loving atmosphere. Even more important, he'd never seen his mother or his father laughing, enjoying each other. They were miserable together. They were miserable—period.

Their form of marriage wasn't for Clay, so he'd chosen carefully. He didn't care if bells didn't ring or stars didn't shoot. Magda was compatible to his needs, and in time he would grow to trust her enough to relax and enjoy whatever their relationship might grow into.

To wait around for a wife because some fleeting emotion called love hadn't hit him over the head was ridiculous. He doubted there was such a thing. What was disguised as love was really the base instinct to mate and procreate. It evaporated as soon as the deed was done. He'd seen it happen often enough.

Confidently he stepped into the hot shower. His decision to marry Magda was right.

MUCH LATER, showered and dressed in his tuxedo, he stood once more at the door of the banquet room, a smile lifting the corners of his mouth as he and Magda greeted his incoming guests. With only a few exceptions, he was happy to see them. Success was in the air.

After everyone had gone through to the large ballroom, Magda gave him a peck on the cheek and whispered that she'd be right back. He smiled absently and patted her hand, his mind on his guests as he tallied those who weren't there yet.

"You've really got them packed in here." David Childers stood just behind Clay sipping on his Jack

Daniels and water. Clay grinned, relieved to see him. David was the one person he could relax with.

"Had to. The list grows. Maybe next year I'll have it at the country club instead," Clay said under his breath. "Glad you got here, though. It's nice to see a friendly face."

"Ah, the price of success." David gave a mocking sigh.

Clay stared at his best friend, his eyes narrowed. He could see what others couldn't. That "Laura ache" was there again. "Where's Laura? You told her to come, didn't you?"

"I don't know where she is. She invited someone else to escort her."

Clay cursed under his breath. "You're really living dangerously, aren't you? You were supposed to bring her."

"I know, Clay. I know." David's voice sounded resigned. He was apparently kicking himself too hard to be able to stand Clay kicking him, too.

Clay didn't say any more. Now wasn't the time to go into it. Ordering a drink from the waiter, he gave David a commiserating squeeze on his shoulder before beginning the long circular path around the room, greeting a few people he had missed at the door and making sure everyone was having a good time.

The band began playing a seductively slow number, and he watched many of the older couples get up to dance, draping their arms around each other in much the same way they had probably done in college. He gave himself a pat on the back for the choice of the band. Just the right blend. Not too old-fashioned, but not too modern, either. Everything was going smoothly.

A streak of brilliant red flashed by the corner of his eye, and he turned in that direction as if drawn. Standing by the hors d'oeuvres table was a petite woman-girl whose long red hair rivaled the brilliance of the dress she wore. A bright emerald-green blouse and full skirt combination in some shiny and questionable fabric, came to just above a pair of very shapely ankles. His eyes moved back up again. Her small plate was piled high with all kinds of goodies, her hands moving almost quicker than the eye as she chose a jumbo boiled shrimp and stuffed it directly into her puckered mouth. Full lips. Wide eyes—he couldn't see the color from here, but he'd bet they were green. Slender to the point of being thin. Trim ankles and high heels that looked as if she was barely able to totter in them. Who was she?

He frowned as he watched her pop another plump shrimp into her mouth. When she tilted her head back he saw the flash of green stones dressing her small earlobes. His gaze narrowed, focusing on the teasing gleam that shone through her mane of red hair. Whether they were great fakes or the real thing he wasn't sure, but he could tell they were perfectly suited to her—even from this distance.

He scanned the room, searching for a possible escort. No one came forth or was paying her the slightest attention.

A guest claimed him, but Clay promised himself that later he would find out who she was. He didn't question why. He didn't have time, as he was swept into a debate on Texas teams by a client who was a football addict.

A half hour later he was ready to leave his own party. Magda had returned to his side and wound her arm through his, lightly clinging to him while graciously discussing the pros and cons of a particular hairdresser with one of his customers' wives.

Terrific. That's exactly why he needed a wife—someone to handle the other half of most couples he had to deal with. She was doing a great job and he said so with his eyes. She smiled back, telling him silently that she expected a reward for her services. He grinned.

She even looked the part. Her dark hair was drawn into a very distinctive roll at the back of her head, showing off her aristocratic bone structure. Her slim body was encased in a smoke-gray dress that molded to her hips and breasts while leaving the impression of long legs. Understated elegance. The doubts he experienced in her absence about his choice of wife disappeared with her next to him.

Excusing himself from both her and the group, he began to circle again, and again a flash of red caught his eye.

The redhead was seated at an inconspicuous table in the back corner of the room, right in front of the kitchen doors. Her crumb-laden plate sat in front of her. One of the young waiters stood by her side holding a glass of champagne, his grin positively lecherous.

Clay angled through the tables, his eyes never leaving her face.

"Really," she explained patiently. "I only wanted a glass of water. That can't be *too* hard, can it? Even truck stops serve water with their chili and chicken-fried steak, for Pete's sake."

"But—" the waiter began.

"What's the matter?" Clay asked quietly.

The waiter seemed to hesitate and Clay could tell that he was looking for an excuse for his actions. "The lady asked for a drink and I brought her champagne. Now she says she wants water." He saw the hard glint in

Clay's eye and reacted quickly. "I was just going to get it, sir," and he scurried off toward the bar.

"My heavens." The little redhead's voice held something akin to awe. "I think he wanted a tip for *water*!"

"Probably," Clay said cynically before diverting his attention back to the girl in front of him. "Is everything else all right?" He slipped into the seat next to her. Her eyes were green all right, almost exactly matching the color of the stones that graced her ears. The widest, greenest green he had ever seen. He could get lost in that brilliant sea-grass green....

"I'm fine, thank you." Those eyes also held a hint of humor. Her voice was soft and sweet, the sounds of a Texas accent rolling around him. "Nice party, don't you think?"

Her words barely registered. He was wondering why he was here at her table, instead of calling someone to quietly escort her out. She was obviously a party crasher— Then her comment registered, and Clay tried not to grin too widely. "Not bad," he agreed. "Do you know many of the guests?"

Her eyes darted away, then came back matched with a delightfully impish smile that seemed to hold him in her spell. "Oh, a few. But there's no use talking to them here. I run into them all the time, you see. We're always attending the same parties."

Clay's grin became broad. She was lying through her teeth, but he was having fun listening. "And do you know Clay Reynolds?" he asked softly, unable to keep from baiting her.

"The man who's giving the party?" she guessed. "I see him occasionally, but he doesn't get out much, does he?"

"He's old, is he?"

Her hand dusted the air. "Oh, sure. But you know how those guys are. Entertainment is a must. Money buys anything."

"I see." Hiding the laugh that wanted to burst out, he waved to the waiter and signaled for his own drink to be brought to him. It came quickly, along with the girl's glass of water.

"Do you live here in San Antonio or are you part of the Austin bunch?" Clay asked.

"Oh, I'm from Austin," she said, jumping at the clue. "I'm only in town for the party, you know."

"What's your name?"

Suddenly the breeziness left her, seeping invisibly into the air. He watched with fascination as her carefree expression evaporated to be replaced with something that almost brought tears to his eyes. "Katherine," she said quietly.

"Katherine what?"

"Just . . . Katherine." She stared down at the glass of water in her hand before tilting her chin at him as if he were a windmill. "And I don't really know anyone here."

"I know."

She searched his face. "You're the one giving the party, aren't you?" It was a statement more than a question. Her insight intrigued him.

"Yes."

"And your money paid for the food."

"Yes."

A small smile tugged at her full mouth. "And you're not an old fossil."

"Not on the outside." His lips mirrored hers.

Then the small smile disappeared. Her vulnerable expression tugged at him. "Class act" was all she said before emptying her glass of water. Clay watched her

delve deep inside herself for what shreds of dignity she
had left. She looked him square in the eyes, hers as clear
and clean as a spring-fed creek. "Thank you for not
making a scene. I appreciate it. Really." She braced her
hands on the table and began to stand.

"Where are you going?" His voice was sharp, sharper
than he meant it to be.

Her brows rose haughtily. She might not be a heavy-
weight, but she wasn't afraid to take him on. "None of
your business. I've eaten and now I'll leave quietly." She
stood, then her face went white, highlighting a scatter-
ing of freckles beneath the surface. "Oh, lordy, not
now," she groaned just before gracelessly crumpling
back in her chair and then dropping toward the floor
in a faint.

Clay moved quickly. His arms circled her tiny waist
and shoulders just fast enough to keep her from hitting
her head on the edge of the table. He lifted her to his
chest, and, feeling as if he was carrying a feather, he
strode toward the kitchen doors, hoping no one at the
party would notice anything unusual.

Waiters stood around staring at him, their mouths
slack or smiling knowingly. He wanted to punch each
one, but wouldn't let go of his grip on the girl to do it.
"How do I get the hell out of here?" he growled, holding her even closer to his chest, protecting his small
bundle.

One of the waiters pointed toward a back door.
"Through there."

Following the direction, he came out in the back hall
of the hotel. He hurried directly to the elevators, but the
ride up to his room was the longest he had ever taken.
He maneuvered his load carefully when he reached his
suite door so he could find his key, then fumbled with

the lock in his impatience. The girl named Katherine moaned, and he cursed under his breath.

Finally the door opened and he strode in, kicking it closed behind him. He carried her through the living room and into the bedroom, placing her gently on the center of the bed before dialing the hotel desk. "This is Clay Reynolds. Please send a physician to my room immediately." The phone landed in the cradle with a snap.

Leaning over her supine form, he brushed the tangle of red hair away from her brow. He searched for some sign of alertness, but there was none.

Her face was heart-shaped. The bones beneath her fair skin seemed almost too fragile to touch and light purple smudges under the golden-brown dusting of lashes showed extreme exhaustion. His fingers brushed her collar and he could feel the birdlike bones underneath. She looked as delicate as a hothouse flower, yet he knew her to be as nervy as they came. He smiled at the picture of her arguing for her glass of water. Apparently she hadn't eaten lately, if the way she was stuffing hors d'oeuvres down her throat was any indication.

Then he spotted the earrings. No wonder he'd been able to see them from across the room. They were exquisite. From the large, perfect, teardrop-shaped emerald hung five rows of small but perfect diamonds held together with golden thread, which now rested against his finger. Bending his head, he looked closer at the intricate webbing of gold. In today's jewelry making, gold wasn't often used with diamonds. If he wasn't mistaken, these earrings were the real thing, not one of the copies that were so plentiful these days.

He touched one, grazing her neck as he lifted the stone slightly and turned it to catch the light. It was a beautiful, clear green stone, its color matching the emerald of her eyes. A gift? Stolen? His curiosity was piqued. Where would a girl like her get expensive earrings like those? A lover who tired of her, but not before gifting her with these? No. They were too expensive even for that.

When the knock on the door came, he jumped, guiltily pulling his hand away.

The doctor was a guest of the hotel, on vacation with his wife. He was kind, a little harried and very quick in his examination. Clay stood quietly by the bedroom door, waiting for him to finish. He had given the man all the information he had.

Katherine's eyelids fluttered, stopped, fluttered again, then opened. "Who are you?" Her voice was strong. Definite.

"Dr. Grossman," the older man said as he smiled down at the woman, and Clay's stomach tightened. The old man had no right to look at a young girl that way. But the physician was apparently not paying the slightest attention to Clay's silent signals. "How are you feeling right now?"

"Sleepy. But not hungry." She smiled back, warm and friendly as a puppy. She hadn't looked at Clay that way and it irritated him.

"I don't think you've been taking care of yourself very well lately, have you?"

"Not hardly." Katherine's voice was full of dry self-derision.

The older man pinched her arm, then watched closely. "You need rest, good food and lots of water. You're slightly dehydrated." The doctor replaced the stethoscope in his bag.

"Of course," Katherine said with mock subservience. She was becoming more awake with every minute. "I'll take care of it immediately."

Her dry sense of humor flew directly over the doctor's head. He snapped the small black case closed. "Good."

"Are you sure that's all that's wrong with her, Doctor?" Clay asked, stepping into the room. His hands were clenched in his black tuxedo pockets, his eyes boring into hers.

"Pretty certain. But you might have her get a complete checkup." He stood and straightened his suit coat around his portly frame. "Until then, let's see what rest, water and good food will do."

With golden-brown eyes Clay stared down at Katherine, and she stared back, her eyes widening as she realized that he'd been here all along. Her heartbeat accelerated under his gaze. She glanced around the room. Expensive. His food, his room, his doctor. When would he call *his* police? She sighed in resignation. Whenever it was, she was ready. She was too exhausted to go one step further without help—anybody's help—including the handsome but stern-faced man at the door who seemed to be in complete control as he paid the doctor off. With cash. Deeper in debt.

He turned and left the room to show the doctor out.

She sat up as the outer door softly closed. Brushing her tangled hair away from her face, she waited for him to come around the corner where she could see him. She needed to try to read his expression so she could guess what he was going to do next. The alternatives were as varied as her scattered thoughts.

Then he was there, a frown on his brow barely hidden by the golden-streaked hair that fell forward to be impatiently brushed back by a long lean hand. He was a golden and brown man, made up of all the warm shades in between.

"Who are you?" he asked abruptly.

"I told you. Katherine. Who are you?"

He ignored her question. "Katherine who?"

She shrugged. "I haven't decided yet."

"What does your birth certificate read?"

"O'Malley," she mumbled, her bravado gone in an instant.

"Well, Katherine O'Malley, what am I going to do with you?"

Again she shrugged her shoulders, but her eyes drifted down to the spread that covered the bed. She didn't want to cry. Not yet. Not in front of him. Not in front of anyone.

His next abrupt question brought her gaze back to him. "Do you have a place to stay?"

"No."

"Are you from here?"

"No."

"Where, then?" he persisted.

She sighed wearily. "Does it matter? Just do what you're going to do and get it over with."

"What do you think I'm going to do?"

His tone was almost conversational, and irritation rose in her. He was playing with her. "Either call security and have me thrown out, or call the police and have me picked up."

"Neither, little girl," Clay drawled, just as the phone rang. He muttered an expletive through his clenched teeth and walked to the small nightstand. "Hello," he barked.

Katherine cringed for the person on the other end of the line. She commiserated with the caller, knowing that she was next in line to be on the receiving end of his temper. If he wasn't going to have her kicked out, did that mean that he expected payment? Judging from her clothes and circumstances, he had to know that she didn't have a dime in her pocket. That meant he had to ask for payment by the age-old barter system. But that type of barter wasn't an option for her. . . .

"I'm sorry, but it couldn't be helped. I'll be down in just a few minutes. Meanwhile, keep everyone happy for me, okay?" His voice had changed from angry to cajoling. Katherine recognized the tone. He wanted something and he was going to get it just by asking. "Good girl," he said, his voice laced with satisfaction. "See you soon."

He hung up and golden-brown eyes once again focused on her. She stared back. He was the first one to retreat, turning his gaze to the small hands in her lap. They were well formed, but with broken nails and calluses. Worker's hands. She thought about hiding them, then decided against it; it was too late.

"Where are you from?"

She shrugged again. "Everywhere."

"The name of the town." His voice was crisp, his attitude one of an attorney with a hostile witness.

She cocked her head at him, her green eyes shining brightly. "You don't give up easily, do you?" she asked.

A small smile tugged at the corners of his mouth. "No."

She sighed. "I'm not telling you," she said simply. "It's my business."

"And now it's mine."

"No." She shook her head in contradiction, her eyes showing just a glimpse of the pain she was feeling. "It's still my business. Your business is deciding what you're going to do with me."

The smile he had been holding back finally broke out. So did a deep, dark, wonderful chuckle that flowed through her body. She couldn't help smile back. "All right, Katherine. You win," he said, but the glint in his eyes told her otherwise.

"Where did you get the earrings?"

His change of subject confused her for a moment, but then her eyes hardened. She touched each ear as if confirming her jewelry was still where it belonged—attached to her ears. "None of your business, but I didn't steal them. They were given to me. In love."

He grunted, refusing to admit he didn't like her answer. If he was right and those jewels were real, they were worth a small fortune. It didn't make sense that she'd wear an outfit that came off the rack of the cheaper clothing stores and then wear earrings that were worth the equivalent of the price of a Mercedes. Perhaps she was lying? He didn't think so, but he couldn't be sure. . . .

Picking up the phone, he called room service and ordered soup and a sandwich, a pitcher of iced tea and their best, most fattening, dessert. When he hung up she was still staring at him. "You don't like what I ordered?"

She nodded, reluctant to believe in her good fortune. "It's perfect, but I'm already stuffed. Why are you doing this?"

He stared down at her, his hands back in his pockets, straining the black material across his muscled thighs. Finally he walked toward the door, his voice so low she almost didn't hear it. "Damned if I know." When he reached the door he turned around and cleared his throat. "My shirt's on the bed. Use it for a nightshirt. Take a bath, eat, then get some sleep. We'll talk in the morning. If you need anything, call the desk and they'll get it for you."

"And where are you staying?" Her green eyes were steady as she looked at him. Hundreds of offers of the same kind put this one in its proper perspective. No one ever gave something for nothing. She'd learned that the hard way. She wasn't upset; she wasn't even disappointed. Just curious. What were his plans and what method of payment did he think justified his care?

"I'm sleeping in the living room. Don't worry, little one. You're safe until the morning, when I grill you again. If you need me for anything, give a call down to the desk and they'll find me. Meantime, enjoy yourself, but stay in the suite."

"I will," she promised softly, earning another puzzling look from him. But where else did he expect her to go, she wondered. If she had had a place, she'd have already been there, not crashing parties so she could grub snacks that wouldn't qualify for bird food.

He hesitated another moment, then turned and slapped his hand against the doorjamb. "Good night."

"Good night," she repeated to no one. The door had already closed quietly behind him.

2

CLAY GAVE A TUG on his cuff links as he strolled back into the ballroom and glanced around at the guests still having a good time. It seemed that none of them—except Magda—had been worried by his absence.

Magda nodded, her eyes narrowing on him as she stood near the band, apparently in a discussion of hors d'oeuvres with the head waiter. It was part of her job to ensure that the table was never empty of its tidbits. Evidently she was more than capable of handling it. Later he would answer for his absence.

He was making his way toward a group of men engaged in a heated discussion when he spotted Laura, her blue eyes glistening with tears as she watched David's back in retreat. He immediately changed his course to head for her, seeing Laura as the solution to the problem of the girl upstairs. His friendship with Laura went back so long that he couldn't remember a time they weren't friends, and he trusted her implicitly.

"May I have this dance?" he asked quietly, taking in the light traces of her tears.

She turned to face him, her hand clinging to his as she nodded. "Please," she said huskily.

Clay slipped his arms around her and began edging his way toward the center of the dance floor. The band was playing a slow number that was almost as many years old as their friendship—years that had gone by too fast in the past and would probably speed up even more in the future.

"David get to you again?"

She nodded, her mouth pressed against his jacket.

"Did you give him a good swift kick in the you-know-what?"

That brought a tremulous smile. "You used to be able to say that word in front of me."

He grinned back, looking down at her with eyes that twinkled, but still showed his concern. "That was when I was young and brash and without taste."

"Ohh." She pretended to be awed at how far he'd come. "And now you're such a man of the world and second only to James Bond in style and panache."

"Something like that," he said, twirling her around. "But occasionally even I don't have all the answers, and have to ask favors from others."

Her smile slipped. "If it has anything to do with David, I'm sorry. . . ."

His arm tightened. "Nothing to do with David, I promise." He could feel her slim body sag with relief, underlining the tenseness that seemed to invade her very skin. "I need help with a dress. Something sedate and too small for you."

Her brows shot up. "What?"

He sighed. "If you promise not to laugh, I'll tell you about it," he said, hoping to distract her enough to smile a little.

"With a teaser like that, how could I resist? Tell all, Clay. I'm hanging on your every word." A smile lit her face.

He explained about Katherine O'Malley, stretched out upstairs in his room, and how she got there, earning more than one chuckle from Laura as he unwound the tale. "And so she needs something that isn't quite so flamboyant if I'm supposed to get her out of here early in the morning and send her on her way. Think you can help?"

She chuckled. "Your problems are solved. Just inside my door is a brown paper bag filled with clothing I was going to drop off at Goodwill. There's bound to be one or two dresses that might fit. Most of them are loose sun dresses that I've had for a hundred years and don't wear anymore."

He gave a relieved sigh; he'd come to the right woman. "Thanks. Can I send my car over and pick them up now?"

"Sure. You know where the key is." No matter how many times he and David had lectured her during the past two months, she continued to leave an extra key to the front door in a plant hanging on the porch.

The band slid from one slow song into another and Clay continued to dance with Laura, intent on getting everything straightened out. "Thanks. It shouldn't take more than half an hour." He glanced up to find two men glaring at him. "By the way, who's the tall guy with the Yuppie look who's been hanging around you?"

"You obviously aren't talking about David."

"Obviously," Clay agreed dryly. "He lives in shorts and knit shirts. It's the other one, over by the table."

She hesitated just a moment, not bothering to look over her shoulder. "Bob Hardy. He works with me and I asked him to escort me tonight."

"Why didn't you ask David? He would have loved to have brought you."

"No." She shook her head, that vulnerable lost look returning to her blue eyes. "He was supposed to be escorting Petra."

"I doubt that. He hasn't seen her in weeks."

"Really?" She gazed up at him, hope daring to shine in her eyes, and he felt a wave of protectiveness flood through him. She hadn't had it easy these past ten years, and occasionally it showed. Her marriage had been rocky at the best of times and finally ended in divorce just before she returned to San Antonio. The experience had taken its toll, robbing her of self-confidence in personal relationships while allowing her to be a bear in business. "He was dating her when I returned here. Everyone told me so."

Clay ignored that. "And when he was dating Petra, he never leaned against a wall and shot daggers at his best friend for dancing with her."

Laura stiffened in his arms. "Is he doing that now?"

"Yes," he chuckled. "So smile and pretend you're having the time of your life."

"It doesn't matter. He's not mad because I'm dancing with you. He's angry with me for dating a man he doesn't like."

Clay hesitated, then decided to plunge in. "How do you know it isn't because he wants to be in Bob's place?"

Laura tilted her head up to look at him, an inexplicable sadness in her eyes. "It's really over, Clay. Best friends can't always fall in love."

He sighed, remembering a long list of regrets that bound both of them to memories better left in the past, and held her closer. "I had that feeling, but I was rooting for you both."

"So was I. I guess we weren't really compatible or ready."

"Ready for what?" Clay asked, a thousand alternative answers springing to his mind.

"Ready to face the fact that lust isn't love."

"Lady, I can imagine a lot of things you two weren't ready for, but those two emotions never came to mind." Love. Lust. Possessiveness. David probably felt all of those for Laura. After all, the man had loved her for almost as long as he'd known her. . . .

The song ended and Laura pulled away. "Walk me to the table, please," she asked quietly, and he nodded, his mind suddenly elsewhere. Upstairs.

"Thanks," he said, grateful to Laura for helping him out on such short notice. Magda might have been closer to the little redhead's size, but he certainly wasn't going to ask her now. He needed her to help keep things oiled, he told himself, seeking an excuse for his behavior.

After making sure Laura was taken care of, he walked across the room toward the hallway doors, wondering if he should check on Katherine one more time before he sent the driver to Laura's. One part of him said yes, but his logic overruled. He'd give the driver the address, and when the bag was delivered, he'd go upstairs just once more, and check on her. After all, the doctor had examined her and he had ordered food. What more could she possibly want?

It took less than two minutes to give the driver instructions and send him on his way. It took another minute to walk back into the party and look as if he'd never left. It took three minutes to spot another flash of red standing at the doorway, trying to gain his attention—and receiving everyone else's.

Her tiny heart-shaped face mirrored worry. Golden-red hair billowing around her shoulders in buoyant curls, she was bent forward as if to reach across the room to him.

He frowned, excused himself from the conversation he hadn't been participating in anyway and made his way toward Katherine. What the hell was wrong now?

Her relief at seeing him was evident in her expressive face. "I'm sorry for bothering you, Mr. Reynolds, but I wanted to thank you for your kindness before I left."

She took two steps backward into the hallway as he approached closer.

"Left for where?" he demanded.

She shrugged her shoulders, looking everywhere but at him. "I'm not sure. But I can't accept your hospitality any longer. It's not right."

"You can, and you will."

"You don't know me from Mrs. Astor's horse. How do you know I wouldn't steal you blind?"

When he didn't answer, she began to turn. "See. I really can't stay."

"Katherine." It was an order. She stopped, turned and stared at him, seeing the unspoken command in his eyes.

"No," she began, shaking her head only to have him interrupt.

"I'm responsible for you. If that doctor thought for a moment that you were leaving, he'd blame me." He took her shoulders and turned her around. "So you'll march upstairs and get back in that bed."

She balked, casting a furious glare over her shoulder. "I'm not a child, and don't you dare patronize me!"

"I'm not. I'm just telling you what you're going to do until tomorrow."

"No, you're not! I'll do as I damn well please. And whatever it is, it isn't any of your business!"

"The hell you say!" Clay said through clenched teeth. "You'll do what I say or I'll have an all-points bulletin out on you in thirty seconds. It could take a long time to explain those baubles hanging from your little ears when you're wearing a dress that couldn't have cost more than an average meal." His eyes held hers. "The chief of police is right inside. Is that what you want?"

Her green eyes darted over his face, searching for the truth. It must have been there, because her shoulders drooped. "You'll get in trouble for helping me. Your girlfriend, or fiancée, or wife will be terribly angry."

He grinned at her fishing techniques. She wasn't going to come out and just ask him; she wanted him to volunteer information about Magda. Angry wasn't the word he would have used to describe how Magda would react when she found out about his little stray. She might be jealous, possessive, even slightly offended. But she would have to love him to be angry—and she didn't. No more than he loved her. He was amazed at what he was thinking.

"Let me worry about that." He took her arm and practically marched her toward the elevator. "And you'll have to stay in the room until I get there." He slipped her the key and punched the floor number then stepped outside of the elevator, watching the doors hide her sad, waiflike face from his view. For some inexplicable reason he wanted to take care of her. It must be that her tiny size provoked a protective, fatherly part of him into action. It never dawned on him to delve into the threats he'd uttered to keep her there. He just wanted it. Period.

But her face was imprinted between him and the closed elevator doors. He shook his head and shrugged his shoulders as if ridding himself of the image. It didn't work. He carried the image all the way back to the ballroom. Even pasting on a smile that was necessary to greet a few late stragglers didn't detract from his thoughts of her.

LAURA'S DATE stepped in from the large back veranda. The man didn't stop at the table he had occupied earlier, but headed straight toward the front door. Clay watched him leave with a spurt of satisfaction. That jerk didn't need to be hanging around Laura and upsetting David's apple cart. David could upset his own without any help.

It seemed forever before the party began to break up. Finally couples began to leave in groups, each saying how much they'd enjoyed the party. Magda stood at his side, her manner cool and confident, secure in her position in his life. Once when she leaned over to kiss one of the women on the cheek, the engagement ring he had given her caught the light and glittered like a knowing eye. A flash of dread hit his stomach and he turned his eyes away. What in the hell was the matter with him?

When the last guest had left they quickly checked the room to make certain that no one had left anything, then slowly walked out of the ballroom, her arm entwined in his. "It was nice, wasn't it?" Magda said with a sigh as they walked the long, glass-enclosed corridor.

"Perfect," he said, gently squeezing her arm. "And you were a perfect hostess. Thank you."

She gave him a sensuous smile. "You're welcome. But I'm sure you'll find some way to reward me, darling. Perhaps a nightcap?"

He halted in front of the large revolving door, shaking his head ruefully. "Not tonight. I'm beat. If you don't mind I'm going to put you in the car and send you home for your beauty sleep."

She pouted delightfully, but had the grace to give in without arguing, even though he could see the gleam of battle in her eyes. She'd wait until a more opportune time to fight: a time when she would win the war instead of just the battle. "Very well, if you insist."

"I do." He grinned, admiring once more his choice of a wife. "I'll make it up to you," he promised.

He walked her to the limo, gave the driver his instructions and kissed her chastely on the cheek. He was not quite ready to admit he was relieved when he saw the car drive away. A quick look at his watch told him it was almost two in the morning. Sleep was next on the list.

THE LIGHT from the living room spilled across the bed, highlighting a spray of golden-red hair on the pillow he was so ready to use. Damn. Somehow during the tail end of the evening he'd forgotten Katherine was in his bed. He backed away into the living room slowly, stumbled over a paper bag of clothing left by the door and cursed softly under his breath.

Because of some misplaced sense of chivalry, he was supposed to fold himself into a comfortable position on the couch and sleep the rest of the night away.

It was either that or kick the redhead out of his bed. Or . . . share it with her.

He brought himself up short. He didn't need complications in his life. In any form.

The couch didn't look so bad after all. . . .

MORNING CAME when the bellhop knocked on the door with a tray filled with breakfast and a pot of steaming hot coffee. Clay had left a breakfast order to serve as a wake-up call, but had forgotten to change the order to include his "guest."

"Give me another order of this in fifteen minutes," he said as he slipped the waiter a twenty-dollar bill.

"Including the coffee?"

"Especially the coffee."

"Yes, sir." The man grinned as he angled out the door. "Right away."

"Thanks." As the front door locked, Clay walked toward the bedroom door, wondering what to do next.

His clothes and the bathroom were in there. And so was Katherine O'Malley.

His problem was solved when the woman he had been thinking about—dreaming about—stuck her head around the door and gave a spritely grin. "Good morning." Her voice was husky with sleep.

"Good morning. Are you hungry?"

She shrugged a bare, silken shoulder, and his eyes caught the movement, his imagination taking over to create what was hidden behind the door. Did she have freckles other than the small ones that dotted her pert, uptilted nose? Or was the rest of her skin as creamy golden as that one slim shoulder?

He pulled his glance away from her and firmly focused on the food upon the roll-about table. "You should be. Come eat while I get dressed."

"What about you?"

"I'll eat after I take a shower."

"Oh." Her glance darted from him to the couch and back to the food, the green depths of her eyes lighting with the beginning of impish delight. "Aren't you sorry now that you decided to give me the bed? I could have slept there without any problem. After all, I'm much smaller."

He *had* noticed and was irritated with himself for doing so. "I had a good night's sleep," he said blandly, ignoring the thought of her, posed in sleep on that brocade-covered couch. Satin against silk ... "Put some clothes on and get out here before this food gets cold."

"Then can I take a shower after you?"

"Yes," he said, the thought of her naked and slick with soap creating havoc in his mind. What the hell was the matter with him? He was supposed to be playing the part of a knight in shining armor, not the lech of the party! It was irritating to have such a strong sexual reaction to a woman, without being mentally prepared for it. Normally he chose the time and place of his arousal, not the other way around. "Hurry up," he ordered roughly.

The door closed quietly between them, shutting him in a room that minutes before had been filled with sunshine. He poured himself coffee and drank half the cup before he realized he'd scalded his tongue. Slamming the cup down, he opened the drapes, staring out at the view of San Antonio's skyline.

The bedroom door opened behind him, just as someone knocked on the outer door. With a muttered expletive he answered it, knowing it was the bellhop with the extra breakfast, and also knowing that the same young man would stare at Katherine and jump to all kinds of conclusions. But he couldn't very well ask her to disappear as if she were some hooker finishing a morning's work.

He was right. The bellhop's eyes honed in on Katherine and she gave a sunny smile in return. "Well, hello," he said, and she giggled.

"Here," Clay said, stuffing another five in the young man's hand. "Thanks."

"Anytime," he said as he walked backward to the door, his eyes still glued to Katherine's smiling face. "Anytime at all, Mr. Reynolds."

Clay could hardly contain the irritation he felt as he slammed the door in the boy's face. Damn! Some jerks in this world actually sat on their brains!

"More coffee?" Katherine asked, pulling up a chair to the table and pouring herself a cup.

"Yes." He watched the tiniest, flirtiest hands tilt the coffee pot to fill his cup. "I take it half-full."

The pot came up at exactly the right spot, without a drop spilling on the tablecloth. "Okay?"

He couldn't help returning her smile. "Okay."

"Why don't you have a seat and eat your breakfast with me, then take a shower?"

He couldn't resist. She was his guest, almost against her will, so the least he could do was be sociable before sending her on her way. Pulling up the desk chair, he sat across from her and uncovered the plate on his side of the table. "Why not?"

Katherine picked up a piece of toast and lavished it with honey butter. "Do you have many parties? Is that dark-haired girl your wife? No, I guess not or I wouldn't be here. Your fiancée? Your sister? No, not your sister. She doesn't look at you the way a girl looks at her brother. She must be your fiancée or girlfriend." She peeked at him through golden-brown lashes. "Girlfriend?"

He bit into a piece of bacon. "Fiancée."

"Mud flaps," her voice was filled with teasing disappointment. "I should have known."

His eyes darted up. "What?"

"I should have known," she repeated patiently.

"Before that."

Her brows rose, making her look like a child playing the role of an adult. Her eyes were guileless and he almost got lost in the green of them. "Mud flaps?"

He nodded, taking another bite of bacon so he'd have a reason to swallow. She had on the same outfit that she'd worn last night, only now the top buttons were undone to show a creamy expanse of throat and just a hint of feminine softness at the rise of her breasts.

"It's just an expression that keeps me from saying what I really want to." She grinned and her whole face lit up. "I might shock somebody if I said what I thought."

"Try me," he ordered, amazed at how low his voice sounded.

"Well . . ." She leaned forward as if to impart a secret, and she did—there were no freckles on the rise of her breasts. "I was hoping that your fiancée was your girlfriend. That way I'd stand a chance of catching you myself. Then I'd have you and my career and beautiful clothes and live happily ever after!" Her chuckle wrapped around him, enclosing him in its warmth, its promise, its delightful effervescence. He grinned back, the corners of his mind telling him he must look like a besotted fool while the rest of him didn't care.

He answered her teasing with his own. "But wouldn't it be difficult to manage your career and my home and me and all the closets of beautiful clothes? I mean, you've got to be a space scientist or an astronaut. At the very least one of *Fortune 500*'s top executives."

"No." Her smile slipped a little, but determination etched her features. "But some day I'll be a damn good secretary and some up-and-coming young man will be at the top of whatever company because I helped put him there."

He leaned back and stared at her through narrowed eyes. He hadn't known too many women who strived for anything other than the right catch, the right marriage, the right man. Her teasing about money slid over him. It was what he expected from the women he knew. "Are you a good secretary now?"

She bit into a slice of toast, her small teeth tearing it delicately. "Not yet. But I learn fast."

"Then what are you? Right now, that is."

"Up until two weeks ago I was a short-order cook and waitress at my brother's truck stop."

Clay sipped his coffee, not really tasting it. "Then what happened?"

"I quit." It was a simple statement but Clay had a feeling there was an enormous story behind those two words.

"To do what?"

"To come to the big city and see if I could get a job that would train me to be the kind of secretary I want to be."

He dropped the pretense of eating, focusing all his attention on her. "So you go around crashing parties and eating off hors d'oeuvres tables, hoping to meet people who would hire you?" How much was he supposed to believe of this story? "I know this might seem a silly question, but why didn't you ask your brother to send you to secretarial school? It would have been easier."

Her eyes clouded with something that looked like hurt. She tilted her chin in the air. "My father was kind, but not smart. Dad left the truck stop to my brother, believing that men are always able to manage business better than women. And my brother is a sweet love-sick man who believes that girls should be ornaments, or work for their relatives so they can be watched over. After all, most girls don't have the brains God supposedly gave to males." She sighed. "Robbie comes from the same old school as my dad did, only Dad believed that women could become excellent secretaries and it was okay for them to do so. Robbie believes any training for women is a waste of time when they'll probably get married and raise kids anyway." She sighed heavily. "Although I love him dearly, Robbie's really limited in his scope of the world."

"I see," Clay began, still confused. What was wrong with her brother's outlook?

"No, you don't. But it doesn't matter." She ran a hand through her hair, pushing it behind her shoulder to expose one of her earrings. They fascinated him, catching his eye as they swung gently from side to side, caressing her neck. "It took me almost three years to save up five hundred dollars to come here and find work. In fact, it was my father who finally gave me the push I needed to leave. Just before he died, he gave me another hundred dollars and these earrings." She lifted the rest of her hair to give him the full view.

"They're beautiful," he murmured. "And expensive."

She nodded, dropping her hair so that it framed her creamy skin again. "Yes. But the one thing I don't want to do is sell them. My dad found them in a pawn shop in Galveston when he and Mom were on their honeymoon. They had gone down to the harbor and were watching all the ships coming and going. The pawnbroker had told them the jewels were a replica of some earrings that a French nobleman had designed and given to his true love. Later, because of the crest on the back, Dad found out they were the real thing and definitely the most expensive thing he'd ever bought. And for a song, too." She smiled sadly. "Dad used to promise Mom that he'd take her to France one day so she could see where the original owners used to live. She was always fascinated with French history. It seems that some of my ancestors came from France and settled in Ireland during the revolution. When Dad found these earrings he told her they would have to do until he could afford the passage."

"Really?"

She nodded again, her expression sincere in her attempt to explain. "There's a crest on the back of one of the earrings. A mountain peak, beside three stars with a name written below. Montclair. They say you can locate anyone by his crest." She took a sip of coffee.

"The other earring holds initials and a few French words. They're very special."

"Just like your parents."

It was a trite remark, but the sadness on her face made him wish he hadn't reminded her of her loss. "Mom wore them on every special occasion I can remember. She used to laugh and call them her good luck charms, and deep down I think she really believed that." She leaned forward. "Dad used to say he gave them in love and they would always represent his feelings."

"And did your dad ever take your mother to France?"

She leaned back in the chair. "No, they never made it. But it didn't seem to bother Mother that much. She used to laugh and tell me that when I grew up she and Dad would send me to France instead. She used to say she didn't need to see someone else's homeland when she had my father."

"So now you have the earrings. What are you going to do with them?"

She shrugged. "I don't know yet. Dad told me to sell them and use the money for secretarial school, but I can't bring myself to do that."

"What happened to the cash you had?"

Her eyes widened. "This town is expensive! In two weeks the money was gone and no one would give me a chance. The only job they wanted me to take was the one I left. If I did that, I know I'd be stuck there the rest of my life. I'd rather die than do that again." Her voice had grown softer with each word until he could barely hear the last sentence.

But he did hear, and her words slammed into his guts like a fist. "That's ridiculous." His comment was like the snap of a rubber band.

"No. That's life—hard, cruel and true." She stood, her shoulders squared. "But what would you know

about that side of life? You look as if you were born with
a silver spoon in your mouth and had brains enough to
clamp down on it."

"I worked damn hard to get where I am." His eyes
grew cold.

"And you made it." She turned and walked toward
the bedroom door. "I've yet to achieve my goals, and
I'm not even sure how I'm going to do it. But I will. I
swear I will."

"Good luck," he muttered to the closing door, wondering how in hell he'd slipped into this predicament.
Twelve short hours ago, he was planning a party and
was satisfied with his life. Now, for some reason he
couldn't explain, he was aching for something that was
missing. He grimaced. What? Disaster in the form of a
redhead? Complications in the form of lust? To hell
with it. Nothing was worth reorganizing his orderly
life. He was exactly where he wanted to be.

In an hour or so he'd be home, minding his own
business. He'd give the girl a hundred and send her back
on the highway to happiness. She was a survivor, she'd
do okay.

Leaning back he closed his eyes, belatedly wishing for
the sleep he hadn't had last night. He quickly opened
them again, surprised that when he shut out the room
he saw a vision of a redhead with green eyes and a vulnerable mouth. And she had been smiling up at him
from his own bed.

He took another gulp of coffee. The mind played
strange tricks on people when they were tired, and this
was the strangest of all.

He was engaged to Magda, and he would stay that
way. Period. The end.

But then he closed his eyes again and propped his
head against the chair. He had to wait for Katherine to

shower, anyway, he reasoned, so he might as well enjoy it. Didn't doctors say that fantasies were good for the mind? They were certainly playing havoc with his body....

3

THAT WAS IT—he would plead temporary insanity. Besides, this whole experience would be all over in a matter of days and his life would neatly slip back into its normal, everyday pattern. All he had to do was wait his craziness out.

Unlocking the front door of his condo town house, he pushed it open. He was probably suffering from something similar to prewedding jitters. After all, any man could be attracted to a woman while engaged to another. And if he hadn't been attracted to Katherine O'Malley, he'd worry that the first signs of rigor mortis had set in. The problems came only when a man followed his attraction through with actions that would betray his fiancée's trust. But anyone could look....

"It's beautiful," Katherine whispered as if she were in church or a library. She stood just behind him in the two-story entryway and craned her neck to see the inside adobe balcony that ran around the second floor game room, then bent forward to view a small section of the living room. "And it's bigger than the truck stop!"

He grinned. "That's saying a lot."

"The decor is so . . . so . . ."

"Stark?"

"No. Simple—yet elegant."

"Thank you."

"Did you decorate it or hire someone else?" She looked up at him and he could see the genuine interest.

"I did it. Surprised?"

She shook her head and her hair curled around her shoulders, lightly caressing the small collarbones. But her eyes held the delight of a child. "Not at all. I bet you could do anything if you set your mind to it."

He smiled, suddenly feeling like king of the mountain. "It's all right if you walk into the living room. I promise it won't swallow you whole," he teased, his glance taking in her tiny feet planted to the floor as if they were glued there. She still wore those ridiculously high heels, but at least she had on one of Laura's casual sun dresses. It had no waist and fell in multicolored folds all the way to midcalf. It was becoming, but not sensuous.

Her eyes touched his and he held his breath, taking in the beautiful fern-green clearness of them. They were so sweet, so pure, so very very beautiful. But lurking there was also a sadness that seemed to weigh on her slight frame. She reminded him of a wonderland wood sprite who would disappear as soon as the brilliance of the sun filtered through the forest to illuminate the ground.

"Is it as large as it looks?"

"Yes." He cleared his throat. "The main guest bedroom is upstairs."

"And your bedroom?" she asked quietly.

"Off the living room. Downstairs." Was she propositioning him? For one wild second he certainly hoped so. Then he came to his senses.

Her eyes were still locked with his. He could feel a thousand emotions flashing through her, sorting out a myriad of possibilities. Then she smiled, slowly at first, but the heat of it hit his stomach like a laser beam. "Thank you," she said.

He shrugged. "It's only for a while, until you can get on your feet. Besides, Consuela will be glad to have more help," he said, referring to his executive secretary. "She's always complaining about how much she has to do by herself."

"I wasn't speaking about the job," she admonished softly. "I was thanking you for ... everything." With a lightning swiftness that he was beginning to associate with her, she rose on her tiptoes and brushed her lips against his cheek, her hand resting on his shoulder for balance. "Thank you, again." Then her touch and lips were gone, and he was chilled by their absence.

Once Katherine had toured the house, she went upstairs. Clay sat in the living room, looking out at the woods beyond the glass floor-to-ceiling windows that stretched across the back of the house, his whole body tense with expectation as he listened to the soft sound of Katherine's steps as she crossed and recrossed the parquet floor of the guest room.

He didn't know what had made him offer her the use of his home until she was established elsewhere. He didn't even know what he had meant by "elsewhere," but he knew he wanted to help.

Yes, she was beautiful and charming and terribly sexy in her tiny way, but he hadn't offered his support for those reasons. He had helped because, quite frankly, she had touched something deep inside him that he hadn't known he possessed. For lack of a better description he named it a well of compassion for the underdog.

"I'll be collecting stray cats next," he muttered into his can of beer. If David was here he'd know how out of character this action was for Clay. Clay and David and Laura. The three musketeers from the University of Texas. Together they were going to conquer the world....

Well, David was making it big now creating computer programming for major companies with special needs. Clay even used a few of David's tailor-made programs for his own real-estate business.

Clay was doing better than he had dreamed possible, owning one of the largest real-estate conglomerates in the Southwest. He had honed a talent for choosing land that, because of location, would become part of other company's packages when they wanted to expand.

And Laura was on her way to being indispensable to a business world who realized her talents. Just transferred back to San Antonio and now part of the board of directors for a growing retail clothing chain, she was both beautiful and intelligent—a formidable combination.

None of them seemed to have dreams they couldn't achieve.

Was Katherine the same? Or did she merely have illusions that would break her spirit before they came true? He hoped not. He'd admired her spunk; and her drive to succeed almost equaled his. So what harm was there if he helped her along with it a little? After all, just because she was a female didn't mean she couldn't use a male helping hand.

He gulped down the rest of the can and crushed it in his hand. "Liar," he growled, standing up and going to the refrigerator for another.

KATHERINE PACED the floor in her bedroom. The guest bedroom. Clay's guest bedroom. She stopped in front of the dresser mirror and stared at herself. "Katherine Maureen O'Malley. I don't know how you've done it, but you stepped on a beehive and came up smelling like honey, an' none o' the bees 're stingin' you," she trilled. "And what's more, I believe you're in love."

Her smile disappeared. No. That couldn't be true. She didn't know much about love, but living above the truck stop had certainly taught her about lust. She'd seen it all her life. As a child she would stretch across her small bed and stare out the window at the parking lot below, seeing more than a child her age should.

Oh, a few of the guys were great, talking about their wives and playing pool or sipping a brew, but they were the exception to the rule. The life of a trucker was hard, both on him and on his family. And most of the men who stopped at her father's place seemed to have been divorced and were fancy-free, still seeking the perfect woman. Meanwhile, who would care if they fooled around a little? Or if they never strived to be perfect men?

Her brother was no exception. He'd done his share of boasting and doing. Until Uda came along. Uda was a young German girl who had caught him quick and held him fast. She didn't lift a finger, and that ensured that Robbie would be forever busy at work, with no time for another woman.

And Uda had made Katherine's life miserable.

Only her father had had faith in her dreams. Only her father had realized she hadn't begun to utilize her talents or intelligence and probably never would as long as she stayed where she was. Her dear sweet dad had given her his most precious possession: her mother's earrings. With those beautiful earrings and a hundred dollars he had handed her an opportunity to change her life for the better. Then, two weeks later he died in his sleep, believing Katherine's dreams would now be fulfilled.

Now she had to prove his faith in her. She'd show him. She'd show the world, she hoped. Not as confident right now as she had been when she'd left, Katherine needed a respite from the overwhelming tension of the past two weeks. But things would change. And when she had made it big in the secretarial world, she'd find a way to pay Clay back for his faith in her and his help. In the end Katherine would pay off all her debts and make it in her chosen world.

The dull metallic thud of pots and pans banging around reminded her of where she was. Clay Reynolds was downstairs.

Now *there* was an enigma if ever there was one. He was definitely high society and just a touch gruff and extremely arrogant. But underneath he was a pushover. Knowing that, she'd be damned if she'd take advantage of him, especially realizing that his fiancée was going to have a screaming fit when she found out there was another woman living in his home. No. Katherine couldn't hurt him that way.

She sat cross-legged on the bed and stared out the window at the top of the post oaks that were clustered in the backyard. But what else could she do? She had nowhere to go and no knowledge of how to change the path her life had taken. She was plum out of decisions and tired of trying to make sense of the world outside the truck stop.

All she could manage was to hang on for the ride and see where she wound up. She prayed that it would be close to Clay, who was more the top candidate for the Knight in Shining Armor award than he ever realized. . . .

"AND THEN I told her she could keep my damn clothes and that I hoped she'd have better luck selling them than

I did wearing them!" Katherine sat on the dining room chair, gnawing away on the smallest drumsticks she'd ever eaten. They were delicious.

"So you took off, with a landlady holding all your belongings, and decided to head for Austin with a trucker?" Clay asked, fascinated by the story of what had happened before they met. He was also intrigued with her mouth as it moved to form words.

"All except my earrings." She grinned.

"You were wearing them?" he guessed.

She nodded vigorously, choosing another small drumstick from the plate in the middle of the table. "Is this tempura batter?" she asked, and it took him a minute to assimilate the change of topic. He nodded. "It's so tasty." Her small tongue darted out to catch a stray crumb. His eyes followed the movement. "So when I passed the hotel and saw the load of cars, I figured, what did I have to lose by stopping? After all, truckers are always going to Austin, but this hotel might not have the same party next week."

"Weren't you afraid you'd get caught?"

She gave a lithe shrug. "What would they do—kick me out? The good Lord knows, I've been kicked out before."

"What about school?" he asked. "Did you take any business courses or typing classes?"

"Mmm." Nodding, she quickly chewed and swallowed. "I took one year of typing in my freshman year and a general business course that taught the rudiments of filing and office management in my second year." She slipped one dainty finger into her mouth and sucked the juice that shone there.

Clay forced his eyes away from her and took a sip of wine. His stomach tightened at the sight of that small action. It was time to regain control of the conversation and keep his mind on the story at hand. He couldn't remember ever having been so interested in a person before. She was certainly different from anything he was used to. "But if you had this burning desire to be a secretary, why didn't you take more courses?"

She gave a heavy sigh and wiped her hands on a cloth napkin. "Because my father had a stroke and was partially paralyzed, so I dropped out at the end of my sophomore year to care for him while my brother ran the truck stop. My father promised me that as soon as he was able to take care of himself, I could enroll in secretarial school." The sunny smile left her face and was replaced with a terrible sadness. "I didn't know then that he would never recover. After steadily going downhill, he died a month ago."

Silence filled the room as she drifted into memories in which he had no part. He felt sorry for her, knowing that losing both her parents must have been a hard blow to accept. Especially since she seemed close to her family.

"It's too late to worry about it now," she said and sighed. "Now I've got to learn to take care of myself and get the education I need."

"You never finished school?" Clay's brows rose as he placed his glass back on the table.

Her chin tilted. He knew that look—it meant she was going to give him a piece of her mind, right between the eyes. "We are legends. And I did complete high school. I took the GED test and passed. That means that I've got the education equivalent to a high school graduate. I even have a diploma to prove it."

"Legion."

"What?" It was her turn to look confused.

"Not 'We are legends,' like a story, but 'We are legion,' like an army."

She didn't give in easily. "A small point."

He grinned. "Very small," he agreed.

Her green eyes turned stormy. "Well, if it's that damn small, then stop smirking," she snapped.

"I'm not. I'm smiling."

"It looks like a smirk to me." She leaned closer to study his mouth, and his grin widened. He refused to recall how long it had been since he had grinned so much! The fresh scent of her lingered in the air between them, and he sniffed it as if to keep it inside him. "Yes." She nodded. "It's definitely a smirk."

"You're looking for an excuse to argue," he managed to say calmly. "I refuse to do so."

She crossed her arms and he was shocked by his awareness of her breasts. They were outlined against the light cotton fabric—small and pert. A beautiful size and perfectly in proportion to her build....

"And you can quit staring at me. I know I look underdeveloped, especially compared to your... your fiancée," she said, having a hard time getting the hated word out.

His eyes popped open and his head snapped up, a light blush tinging his tanned cheekbones. "That's not exactly polite table conversation."

"Neither is staring polite."

"I wasn't staring."

"And I've got a diploma, whether you think so or not."

She was belligerent. She was beguiling. And he hadn't felt like laughing so much in years. He knew he was rusty, but two could play her game. "And your breasts are beautiful. Just right for you."

Her eyes widened as his comment soaked in. That did it! He was being just as outrageous as she was! Her frown slipped into a smile, the smile into laughter that bubbled from her toes to her throat and echoed lightly in the room.

Then he joined in.

When the laughter died down, their eyes met and held. Silence seemed to slice the room in two, and thoughts tumbled through his head at the speed of light.

"When are you getting married?" she asked softly.

"In six months."

"Oh."

He cleared his throat and sat up straighter. This new relationship had to move to a firmer footing. "I've got an idea about a place you can stay, but I have to check it out. Do you have any clothes that would be suitable in an office environment?"

Katherine sighed. He was back to being aloof again. "No," she admitted. "Unless you count those three sun dresses as suitable."

"What about at that rooming house where the woman is holding your belongings?"

"I have five outfits there, one or two might work, but I don't have the money to bail them out."

"I do," he said, pushing away from the table. "You clean up the kitchen and I'll make a few phone calls." He saw that defiant look wash over her piquant face. She obviously didn't like to be ordered around. "I cooked dinner, remember?"

Reluctantly she nodded.

He left the room as quickly as possible, heading toward his study just off the master bedroom. Breathing space. That's what he needed. Time to get his priorities in order.

Katherine was a nice girl in a bad situation, and he was just helping her out. That was all. He repeated that over and over as he closed the study door and headed for the phone. First he'd get her clothes back and then he'd see about finding her a place to stay. Once that was accomplished, his life would be back to normal and he could give a sigh of relief for completing what he shouldn't have started in the first place.

The rest of the evening passed peacefully. Clay played some tapes on an obviously complicated stereo system that had awed Katherine. He drank another two glasses of wine and read a new spy story that had just hit the bestseller list, but it didn't hold his attention as much as the sprite who was sitting on his couch did.

She was seated in the corner, her legs curled under her. Her eyes were closed and there was a small smile on her parted lips that told him she loved the sound of light jazz almost as much as he did. Where had she acquired the taste for it? Certainly not in a truck stop between San Antonio and the Gulf of Mexico!

Finally he dropped all pretense of reading and watched her openly. If God had made leprechauns, this would be what they had developed into over the centuries.

Her hair billowed around her shoulders like an aureole, her skin was so clear it was almost translucent. Most men he knew would give their eye teeth for a chance to dress her up and parade her in front of others—until they found that they couldn't curb her wayward tongue or her slightly unorthodox attitudes. . . .

Katherine felt the pressure of his gaze, but couldn't gather enough nerve to open her eyes and see his expression. Was he laughing at her or would there be pity in his gaze? She didn't want to know. It was enough to sit here on a couch that cost more than all the furniture in her father's apartment and listen to strange music that had an unusually soothing effect.

He had made a deal with the landlady and was picking up her clothing tomorrow, despite Katherine's protests. Now she not only owed him for his kindness and hospitality, but she owed him money, too. Her smile drooped. But she'd pay him back somehow, if it took her all her life. Katherine Maureen O'Malley would be beholden to no man. It would be an even exchange or there wouldn't be any exchange at all. Except this one time. . . .

The phone rang and jolted her out of her reverie. With the snap of pages slapping together, Clay put the book on the coffee table and headed for his study. Her stomach flipped as his voice changed from a harsh bark to soft chuckles. It must be Magda. His fiancée. That word hurt more than any other she could think of.

It was time to face the fact that she was falling head over heels in love with a man so far out of her sphere that he might as well be on another planet. Try as she might, there didn't seem to be any way to head off the fall she knew was coming. She was all wrong for him, she kept telling herself, but it hadn't stopped her heart from tripping over her head in an effort to love him. Knowing that Cinderella stories had nothing to do with reality didn't seem to help, either.

His voice drifted to her, and even though his words were muffled, the intimacy of his conversation came through loud and clear. He was treating Magda to a lovers' dialogue, and Katherine ached with the unwelcome envy that surged through her body with every vowel spoken.

What was the matter with her? She had no right to infringe upon anyone's life, especially not upon the man who was trying to help her stand on her own two feet! All she would do was hurt herself even more by harboring thoughts that had no place in her life, her situation.

She held herself stiffly against the couch, praying the emotions that flowed through her like an inky dark river would leave quickly. She wanted peace, and with that peace would come contentment. She knew because she'd had it once and had starved for it ever since.

She sighed, leaning her head back on the firm cushion. There hadn't been such a thing as peace in her life since she was a child. At the tender age of ten, she had lost her mother to cancer. She didn't linger and slowly fade away, but was ill one week and gone by the end of the month, leaving a vast and empty hole in all their lives.

Her father had been devastated, barely able to work without being reminded of the large, happy woman who had walked the same linoleum he was walking, cooked the same food he was cooking. She had smiled the same smile he no longer could find in his repertoire of facial features. Oh, her mother hadn't been beautiful or svelte or even outstandingly intelligent. Instead, she was overweight with a face that would have been called Irish-cute in its youth. And she had never understood multiplication. But she had been the very glue with which the family was stuck together. They had all used her as the pivotal point in their lives—the sun they all circled.

When she'd died, their lives and peace and happiness had shattered into a thousand pieces, never to be glued back together again. And since her mother's death, Katherine had been seeking that elusive, comforting security, not knowing exactly what it was, but realizing she would recognize it when she saw it . . .

Right now, she recognized it in Clay, and that was frightening.

He didn't want her. He didn't want to be any more than a friend in need. It was *her* heart that was crying out, not his.

Her best move would be to repay his thoughtfulness guardedly so she wouldn't interrupt his flow of life. She would be the best friend he ever had.

His voice drifted in and out of her thoughts, a sentence here, a chuckle there. She snuggled deeper into the marshmallow-soft couch and gave a small sigh. It felt nice to make her decisions on life before she slept. That way her mind was cleared of problems.

CLAY STARED down at the woman curled in the corner of his couch. She might be as small as a child, but she was certainly all female. He knew because his libido had shouted at him all evening, despite his dire warnings to himself.

Before he went into a trance staring at her, he decided he might as well send her off to bed and head for his own. Tomorrow was supposed to be a busy day, although for the life of him he couldn't remember anything he wanted to do at work. The only item on his list right now was to wrestle Katherine's clothing back from the landlady. Everything else was secondary.

He sat on the side of the couch and brushed a curl away from her cheek. "Katherine," he murmured, wondering where the force of his voice went. Damn! Her name sounded too much like a verbal caress. He cleared his throat. "Katherine!"

She jumped, and he pulled his hand back quickly. Her green eyes widened as she stared at him seated next to her. He smiled. "I'm sorry, I didn't mean to startle you. I just wanted to point you in the direction of your room so you could sleep in comfort."

"Thanks," she said, relaxing and stretching her arms over her head. "I didn't realize I had dozed off."

"You're entitled to. You've had a busy week."

Her eyelids drooped with tiredness, giving her a sensuous look that tingled through him. "I guess I have," she admitted, uncurling to stand in front of him. "I'll see you in the morning."

"Right." His tone dropped two octaves, his golden-brown eyes glued to her.

But he still wasn't expecting it when she bent down and dropped a kiss lightly on his lips. "See you in the morning, Clay."

"Yes. Sure." He watched her walk out of the room and toward the stairs. Her fingers hooked the straps of her shoes, her arms drifting sensuously about her as she swayed across the room, her small bottom swinging sweetly from side to side as she glided barefoot across the thick carpeting.

Cursing under his breath, he turned and stared out at the night, attempting to rid himself of the image of Katherine walking across the room. But the vision was indelibly burned into his mind.

It was over two hours before Clay found his own bed. Another two hours before he could close his eyes without seeing a flame-headed sprite whose green eyes glittered with the promise of sensual dreams and whose touch was as light and airy as stardust.

4

MORNING CAME TOO EARLY, but Clay was forced to greet it anyway. After turning off the alarm clock that he'd set for seven, he heard Katherine in the kitchen. The smell of sizzling bacon wafted under the closed door. He sniffed, stretched, then rested his head against folded arms, imagining her puttering around. A small smile tilted his lips as he mentally watched her going through the motions of cooking breakfast.

She would be in a short T-shirt and even shorter shorts, her golden-red hair held back by a bright green ribbon. In her unusually husky voice she would be lightly humming a tune that would soak into his skin and make his body sing along. Her movements would be graceful and quick, as sensuous as a knowledgeable woman's wiles.

The sound of glass breaking shattered his imagery. Or perhaps she would be as clumsy as a child....

He sighed and pulled himself off the bed. He might as well shower and eat. He had a full day ahead of him.

KATHERINE TURNED the bacon over, humming an old country-and-western tune in a kitchen that was the dream of a gourmet cook. Only she wasn't that kind of animal. Bacon, fried potatoes and eggs with toast or flour tortillas would have to do; she had never learned how to make hollandaise sauce for eggs Benedict. She had a sneaking suspicion, though, that the latter was probably more Clay's style.

She glanced down at the multicolored sun dress she had worn yesterday and had on again this morning. It was faded and not at all flattering, but at least it covered her. Her fingers traced the plait of heavy hair that fell down her back, making certain it was still neatly contained. Wishing had never gotten her anywhere, but once more she wished she had soft, smooth hair, more height and fuller breasts. And not necessarily in that order.

The muffled sound of an alarm clock whispered through the rooms, and she glanced quickly at the large brass-and-glass clock on the far living room wall. He must have set his alarm for seven. It continued to hum for over a minute before it stopped.

She could almost see him, his jaw shadowed with early-morning stubble, his eyes closed, his lashes onyx against his golden-tanned skin. She'd bet he didn't wear pajamas to bed. Light, golden-copper skin would contrast sharply against the white of the sheets. His sun-streaked hair would be ruffled, like a child's, but to her fingers it would feel sensuous. His mouth. His mouth would be slightly parted and warm breath would pass in and out, gliding past his firmly formed lips....

Enough. Her muscles tightened and her nerves sang with tension. She spun around and reached for the fork to take the bacon out of the pan. Instead, she hit the small, half-filled glass of orange juice sitting on the counter. It tilted sideways and, spilling its sticky contents, quickly rolled across the counter and into the sink, breaking with the sharp sound of tinkling glass.

"Mud flaps," she muttered, gingerly picking up the broken pieces and wrapping them in paper towels before dropping them into the trash. This is what she got for daydreaming about impossible quests. Reality wasn't Clay asleep or awake. Reality was a broken glass and sticky counters and floor.

By the time she'd finished cleaning up the mess and salvaging the bacon, water was running in the downstairs bathroom. With fingers that were less than deft, she sliced up the two potatoes she had cleaned earlier, then dumped them into the leftover bacon grease and began frying them. When Clay turned the shower off, the potatoes would be cooked and waiting. Brown eggs sat on the countertop, ready to be broken and cooked to his preference.

She poured another glass of juice and walked to the uncurtained bay window in the small kitchen eating area. There she paused to stare at the forest outside.

It was beautiful in an untamed way. Instead of carefully placed shrubs and immaculately tended beds, there was an abundance of trees crowding all the way up to the deck that ran the full length of the back. The branches created soothing cavelike shadows where mounds of wild fern clustered together for protection. She could see tulips and day lilies gathered here and there in clumps, as if casually dropped rather than carefully planted by someone trying to imitate nature. About halfway back through the yard was a wood and wrought-iron bench that faced the back corner of the woods, inviting someone to sit there and contemplate the wonders of nature.

"Katherine?"

She pivoted, the dress streaking around her calves like a circular rainbow. Her hair flew back to allow a glimpse of richly jeweled earrings gracing small lobes. Her jade-green eyes were wide.

"What is it?" He was standing far enough away from her, yet he knew that if she hadn't been so close to the window, she would have taken two steps back.

"Nothing." She shook her head and the sunlight bounced around her golden-red halo.

"What is it?"

"You startled me."

"What were you thinking?"

Her eyes were wide, unflinching. Honest. "About how wonderful it would be to walk out there in the moonlight. I bet you could catch moonbeams darting through the leafy canopy."

He took a step closer. "Would you like to do that tonight?"

"No."

"Why not?"

She gave the smallest of smiles. "Because I like the way I think it would be better than the way it really would be."

"How do you know?"

That sadness in her eyes again. "I just do."

The silence stretched between them as Clay watched her, his eyes narrowed. She was honest and . . . right.

He had often thought fancifully that moonlight was captured by the shady boughs of the trees. He would sit on the deck with the house lights out and watch the black-shadowed trees bend and dance in the softly playing breeze, listen to the light chatter of leaves talking to each other, and wonder if it was magic.

And so had she.

He took two more steps, towering over her, and a wave of that protective emotion she evoked washed over him. Protect her from what? some far-off part of him asked. Only he didn't have the answer.

Fear and tension were still radiating from Katherine as if she were a thundercloud throwing out the beginnings of a lightning storm. She scooted around him, ducking under his raised arm. "Ready to eat?"

"Eat what?" His voice was a growl. His brows met over the bridge of his nose.

"Breakfast. Bacon, potatoes and whatever kind of egg you want."

He wanted none of the above, but couldn't—wouldn't—say so.

"How do you want your eggs?" she persisted, walking back toward the stove top and reaching for them.

Clay sighed. "Over easy." Eggs would have to take care of the hunger he was barely able to acknowledge himself.

With forced brightness, she smiled. "Over easy it is." But there was still that hint of fear or wariness in her eyes and he wasn't brave enough to pursue the cause.

Clay Settles Reynolds wasn't sure what formed his own fear: how could he help her through hers?

He couldn't say how he had made it through breakfast and then out the door, without uttering more than one or two words. The phone had rung twice and he had let the answering machine pick it up, not wanting to have the outside world intrude upon the silent time before the morning bustle.

Katherine hadn't said much, either, cooking his eggs just right before joining him at the small glass table. When his cup was a quarter empty, she filled it to half full with more hot, steaming coffee. When he ate the last of his toast, she slipped one more piece into the toaster and set a jar of blueberry preserves in front of him. All without asking.

It was uncanny. It was also unsettling, and he reacted by frowning, then glowering at her. He didn't like his mind read so easily, so quickly and so accurately. Instead of making him comfortable, it unnerved him.

He got up, wadding his napkin into a ball, and left, only giving the barest of explanations. "I have some

running around to do. I'll be back in an hour or so."
And he refused to look back to see if her expression was
sad or happy with his leaving. He couldn't have handled the answer, either way.

He drove just south of downtown to one of the old,
run-down neighborhoods, checking the street against
the address Katherine had given him. When he found
it, he stopped the car and stared.

It was a large two-storey clapboard house that had
seen better days twenty years ago. Maybe. Now, ac-
cording to the sign out front, it was divided into rooms
for rent. The porch dipped under the weight of a saggy-
diapered toddler running barefoot along its length. One
window held an air-conditioning unit that obviously
wasn't working or it would have been humming. Faded
white paint was peeled in spots, flaking like the crust
of a pie. The whole structure was a monument to antique engineering. What amazed him most was that it
was still standing instead of crumbling in a cloud of
dust.

He couldn't believe people actually lived in places like
this. And yet this was where Katherine had spent her
past two weeks.

He strode up the cracked and broken sidewalk and
opened the kicked-in screen door, standing for a moment to let his eyes adjust to the dimness inside.

"You want somethin', mister?"

His eyes narrowed, watching the largest lady he'd
ever seen waddle toward him. Her dress was supposed
to be shapeless, but it wasn't. It hugged every curve and
bulge. "I'm looking for Mrs. Adams."

"That's me. What can I do for you?" She examined
him closely, then pursed her lips.

"I came to get Katherine O'Malley's suitcase."

"You got the money?"

He held out an envelope. "I'll give you this as soon as you produce the suitcase."

The large lady shrugged, but her eyes were glued to the envelope. "That's fine. I don't care as long as you pay."

The transaction was over in a minute, then Clay was out the door. It took another minute to swallow the bile that had risen in his throat. Being poor was one thing. Being dirty was a whole different ball game. And that place and its landlady were filthy.

He drove to his office with the car windows down. Grabbing gulps of hot air, he tried to rid his lungs of the putrid stench of the ground-floor apartment he had reluctantly entered.

By the time he pulled into his parking slot, he knew with deep-down determination that no matter what he had to do, he'd never send Katherine out in the world until he was certain she was safe from places like that. No one deserved to live like that. No one.

In the back of his mind was another problem he would have to face—a problem he told himself had nothing to do with Katherine. He had chosen to marry for all the wrong reasons and needed to right the wrong for both his and Magda's sake. It wasn't fair to either of them. It had taken all night to face the fact, but at last he had.

CONSUELA WAS WAITING to pounce on him the minute he walked through the door of his suite of offices. Silently he waited for the Mexican fireworks to explode. Her small stature was deceiving, as were her grandmotherly features. The woman was a miniature dynamo—like Katherine. "I've got three new secretaries to train on the computer this afternoon and no trainer around to do it. Either I call the employment agency for someone to work in here while I train or I'll have to cancel. Which will it be?"

He reached toward the plate of fresh cookies that always sat next to the coffee pot: Consuela brought something different every day. "What has to be done here?"

Her back was still rigid. "Mainly answering the phone, typing a few invoices, some filing."

He chewed on the cookies, tasting coconut and butterscotch. Not bad. "I'll take care of it."

Consuela's brows rose in the air. "You? You've got a business meeting at two o'clock. How are you going to do two things at one time?"

"I think I know someone who can fill in for you for a while. You'll be training her in office work next week anyway. Might as well start now."

"A girl?"

Clay nodded, unable to look at her as he reached for the stack of mail set aside on her desk.

"Someone I know? I interviewed?" Consuela was nothing if she wasn't persistent.

"No. A friend. Katherine O'Malley. She needs a job and I thought of letting her help you out."

"Really? Then why didn't you tell me about her before?"

"Because I just found out," he sighed, wondering why she always sounded like a mother. It must have been conditioning at an early age, since she had seven of her own brood to care for.

"Is she a nice girl?"

Clay's eyes twinkled. He'd never before hired a girl he knew. "She's very nice and needs a job. I offered, knowing that you've got your hands full already and were dying for extra help."

There was only the hum of the air conditioning in the outer office as his secretary digested that fact. Then she sighed heavily. "I'll take the help." Consuela granted her seal of approval as if he'd asked for it.

"Good. I'll bring her here after lunch."

She nodded. "By the way, boss. Those cookies are called spell-breakers."

He raised his brow.

She grinned. "I thought you'd need some."

He should have known. Consuela and Magda had never gotten along.

The mail was handled quickly and efficiently, with Clay jotting notes for some and dictating longer answers for others. He and Consuela worked well together, completely organized and in tune.

He wished the day would continue this way, but he knew better. As long as he kept working and busy, he wouldn't be able to think, to puzzle over the flame-haired woman who had entered his life and brought on more complications as each hour passed. She was a wildflower, and he wasn't a very good gardener.

But if he kicked her out, she might wind up in another dump like the one he had just left. What chance did she have of bettering herself if she was stuck in a place like that?

No. He had to help her. He'd put Katherine back on her feet and consider his Christian duty done. Then he could get on with his life.

With an expression of smug satisfaction on his face, he reached for the phone.

"WHY IN THE HELL didn't you answer the phone if you heard me calling to you?" Clay ran a hand through his hair, his frustration plainly visible as he stood next to his desk at home.

"Because you mentioned that you had the answering machine on and I didn't know if I would mess it up if I stopped a recording," she explained, equally frustrated.

"You don't have to stop the recording. You just pick up the phone and wait until the message is over."

Her hands rode belligerently on her hips. Her toes were almost even with his as she craned her neck up to glare into his face. "And how am I supposed to know that? I've never even *seen* one of those things before!"

The fight left him. "Okay, okay. I didn't realize that. I thought . . ." He let the rest of his sentence drift off, realizing just how snobbish it sounded.

But she finished it for him, her voice dripping with sarcastic sweetness. "You thought *everyone* knew how to operate such a simple piece of equipment." Anger flashed in her green eyes. "Well, I'm sorry, sir, but truck stops don't have answering machines. Nor do the trucks. But I can work a restaurant gas grill or a citizen's band radio better than you ever dreamed of doing!"

"And if I need help on a CB, I'd call you, but the chances of that happening are slim!"

Her breath was warm on his lips as she reached up on tiptoe, almost touching his nose with hers. "Just teach me, dammit, instead of griping about it!"

He did, explaining the procedure of answering calls and listening to recordings. Katherine's lowered head as she followed the steps almost made him smile, but he didn't want to lose the anger that had so recently boiled through him. Anger between Katherine and himself was a lot safer than other emotions.

By the time they were in the car and driving back to the office, he had cooled down and the only obstacle he could drum up to put between them was silence. He

What is sexy?

Jōvan® Musk.

What sexy is.

SAVE UP TO $2.00
FOR YOU <u>AND</u> THE MAN YOU LOVE
ON JŌVAN MUSK!

SAVE $1.00
JŌVAN® MUSK
FOR MEN

TO THE RETAILER: For each coupon you accept from the customer at time of purchase of any Jōvan Musk for Men item, Jōvan will pay you $1.00 plus 8¢ handling if terms of offer have been complied with by you and the consumer. Presentation for redemption without such compliance constitutes fraud. Payment will be made only to retailers stocking these products. Invoices proving purchase of sufficient stock to cover coupons presented for redemption must be shown upon request. Coupons may not be assigned or transferred. Any sales tax must be paid by the consumer. Offer good only in the U.S.A. and void where prohibited, licensed, taxed or restricted by law. Cash value 1/20 of 1¢. Unauthorized reproduction of this coupon is prohibited. For payment, mail coupon to Jōvan, Inc., P.O. Box 14851, Chicago, Illinois 60614. **Offer expires 3/31/89. Consumer Note:** Limit one coupon per purchase of any Jōvan Musk for Men item. **Consumer must complete information below to redeem coupon.** This information will be kept confidential.

NAME _____

ADDRESS _____

CITY _____ STATE ____ ZIP _____

MANUFACTURER'S COUPON – EXPIRES 3/31/89

H

5 35017 12276 1

SAVE $1.00
JŌVAN® MUSK
FOR WOMEN

TO THE RETAILER: For each coupon you accept from the customer at time of purchase of any Jōvan Musk for Women item, Jōvan will pay you $1.00 plus 8¢ handling if terms of offer have been complied with by you and the consumer. Presentation for redemption without such compliance constitutes fraud. Payment will be made only to retailers stocking these products. Invoices proving purchase of sufficient stock to cover coupons presented for redemption must be shown upon request. Coupons may not be assigned or transferred. Any sales tax must be paid by the consumer. Offer good only in the U.S.A. and void where prohibited, licensed, taxed or restricted by law. Cash value 1/20 of 1¢. Unauthorized reproduction of this coupon is prohibited. For payment, mail coupon to Jōvan, Inc., P.O. Box 14851, Chicago, Illinois 60614. **Offer expires 3/31/89. Consumer Note:** Limit one coupon per purchase of any Jōvan Musk for Women item. **Consumer must complete information below to redeem coupon.** This information will be kept confidential.

NAME _____

ADDRESS _____

CITY _____ STATE ____ ZIP _____

MANUFACTURER'S COUPON – EXPIRES 3/31/89

H

5 35017 12376 8

We'll provide a fascinating, handsome hero or four. You'll find them on our incredibly sensual new covers, starting this month.

We'll make it all so easy. All you have to do is read and dream of that special moment when you abandon yourself to Temptation. Collect your 2, 3 or 5 Harlequin Temptation tokens, fill in the coupon below, and send the tokens and the coupon with your check or money order to Harlequin—your nightshirt will arrive before the last kiss is even faded from your memory!
Offer ends December 31, 1988.

And we'll show you a way to share the moment with the one you love.
The finishing touch is on the next page: an offer on deliciously provocative fragrance that adds to the fantasy— for you and your man....

pulled the car into his parking slot and turned off the engine, making no move to leave the confines of the car. Katherine waited expectantly, knowing she was about to receive last-minute instructions and hating it. Did he think she was a complete fool? Obviously.

"My secretary, Consuela, is a wonderful woman, but she has a mothering instinct that began when she was an infant herself. Please bear with her. She'll probably repeat everything a thousand times, but she means well."

Her slow smile lit up her face. "I will."

Clay stared at her for a moment, then nodded his head. He reached for the door handle wondering who would explode first, his secretary or his houseguest. He couldn't imagine.

"Clay?"

He turned reluctantly to the wood sprite beside him when her hand reached out to touch his sleeve. "I'll behave. I promise."

Her touched warmed his skin, and he sighed heavily with regret. Who was he to tell her she wasn't behaving properly? He was the one engaged and entertaining a female houseguest at the same time!

By the end of the day he was acting like a bear with his paw in a trap. From the moment Consuela and Katherine had met, his secretary had behaved as if Katherine were one of her wayward children returning home. Every time Consuela glanced at the younger girl, her eyes lit up with something he couldn't put his finger on, but didn't trust. He was as wary as hell and he didn't know why.

Katherine pored over the letters that needed to be filed, her brow knit in consternation.

"Don't worry. The files are set up by company, and you just need to check each company name and place them in the proper files, the latest dated letter first," the plump secretary said, giving Katherine a pat on the shoulder. "Just take your time and you'll catch on."

"You think so?"

"I'm sure so." Consuela was nothing if not an optimist. "What you need to remember is which phone goes to which office. I've written down the codes here. See?" She pointed to a sheet of paper stuck to the side of the phone console. "Just make sure you put the caller on hold before you switch over, or you'll lose them."

"Right," Katherine said, wondering how she would get used to doing all this as efficiently as Consuela seemed to. This was certainly nothing like slinging hash! She straightened her spine. She could do it. She could do anything.

By the time Consuela had left for a training session, Katherine was posted behind the desk and ready to handle anything that came her way.

The calls were dispatched with efficiency, so much so that she was polishing her nails on her shirt with pride. Until almost closing time . . .

When the phone rang, Katherine answered, her voice clear and secretarial crisp. "Reynolds Corporation."

"Let me speak to Clay, please." The female voice on the other end of the phone definitely had a proprietarial edge.

"May I ask who's calling?"

"Magda, his fiancée. Who's this?"

"This is Miss O'Malley."

"Oh." Distant interest laced the caller's voice. "Are you new there, Miss O'Malley?"

"Yes." Katherine's brightness belied the heaviness in her stomach. "I just began today."

A throaty laugh emitted across the line. "Good luck with Consuela. Would you put me through to Clay now, please?"

"Certainly," Katherine responded in what she hoped was her most businesslike voice. "Please hold."

Then she quietly laid the phone back in the cradle and disconnected the line. A smile curved her lips, genuine but slightly guilty.

"Who was that?"

Jumping at the sound of his voice, Katherine darted a glance toward Clay's door to find him lounging against the jamb. "It was, ah, a woman, but I forgot to push the Hold button. I think I lost her."

His brows knitted together. "That was careless, Miss O'Malley. Very careless."

She tried to look repentant. "Yes, sir."

When the phone rang again, she jumped again. There was nothing wrong with her intuition—it was screaming that the woman she had hung up on was calling back.

Clay strode across the room, picking up the receiver with more energy than was necessary. "Reynolds Corporation."

Katherine's green eyes looked everywhere but at Clay. She fiddled with the papers she had been filing, stacking them in neat, inconsequential piles. She could feel Clay's eyes boring into her, but she refused to glance his way.

"We have a new girl today, and she's just learning the procedures," Clay answered to a barrage of words. She could hear the voice, but couldn't make out what Magda was saying. Her stomach tightened.

"I know. And I'm anxious to see you, too." Clay's voice had softened and it was like dark liquor running over thick cream.

Standing, she pretended to sort through the letters once more and ready them for filing in the cabinets behind her.

"We need to talk," he said, his voice even more husky, and Katherine's mind went wild imagining what he was referring to. She knew, but couldn't admit it. She just couldn't.

"About eight."

Her hands clenched the letters into a mangled pulp, her eyes finally turning to lock with his. A flash of lightning passed between them, jolting her with its force before he looked away. "See you then."

The silence in the office was almost earsplitting. Neither moved as they waited for the other to act, to say something, to break the spell.

"Don't do that again."

"I'm sorry."

"Just don't do it again."

She shook her head slowly. There was a sheen on her green eyes that made them look like highly polished, very coveted emeralds. "No," she whispered. "I won't."

His mouth moved once, as if he were about to say something. Then he changed his mind, turned and strode back into his office. But not before he'd stolen the last cookie from the plate by the coffeepot. The door shut behind him quietly, but it could have been a shout the way it grated on Katherine's nerve endings.

With a sigh she plopped into the desk chair, her hands still clutching the papers. She had to get a hold on herself before she upset two lives: his and hers.

5

IT WAS AFTER MIDNIGHT when he returned from Magda's house. All the way home, his head had been throbbing. He'd been trying to do too much, push too hard; now exhaustion was setting in. At least that's what he told himself.

He'd worked until minutes before his eight-o'clock date with Magda, then tiptoed his way through a broken engagement. It hadn't been an easy decision to make, but he knew it was the right one. He didn't care for her enough to spend the rest of his life with her. It wasn't her fault. And it wasn't his.

Slipping the key in the door, he stepped into the hallway. The house was in darkness except for one small lamp on the Bombay chest in the living room. He walked in, peering over the back of the couch.

A country-and-western waltz played on the stereo, barely audible. Dim golden light danced over the room as if playing hide-and-seek.

But his eyes were trained on the couch. Katherine was curled up in the corner, her hair cascading over the side like a molten, golden-red waterfall. Her chin rested sweetly against a throw cushion that was pressed against her body and held tightly in her arms. Her golden-brown lashes, unadorned by makeup, rested against the creamiest skin Clay had ever seen. For just an instant, he thought of the rest of her body having that same golden-white tint. His hands curled into fists.

Enough of looking into the jaws of temptation.

"Katherine, it's time to go to sleep," he said loudly. The incongruity of his words hit him at the same time as she raised her eyelids and smiled.

"It makes sense to me," she yawned.

She held out her hand and he pulled her up, then dropped his own arms to his side quickly. Katherine's smile was slow and dreamy—and extremely sexy. That exhausted feeling he'd had just a short time ago disappeared.

"Good night, Clay," she mumbled, waving slowly as she made her way toward the staircase. "Sleep tight."

"Good night," he finally ground out. What a thing to say to a man who was watching the sway of the most delectable derriere he'd ever seen. 'Sleep tight' just about summed it up!

He aimed his steps toward the wet bar in the corner and poured a crystal balloon glass of golden-colored brandy, then sank down in the same spot Katherine had just vacated. The heat of her body still clung to the cushions, warming him more than the brandy. Her scent hovered in the air, lightly invading his senses and making him even more aware of her presence in his home.

Deliberately closing his eyes, he leaned his head back and tried to relax. Instead his body hummed with tension. His eyes popped open, dispelling the fantasies he knew were waiting to claim his sleeping hours.

Katherine was nothing more than a friend in need. She was a friend, and a well-rounded man needed both male and female friends.

He would make himself into a girl's best friend and nothing more. He'd help her as much as he could, then walk away when her need of him was over. He'd be damned if he'd allow that wisp of a girl any more leeway with his emotions. Katherine would not be any more to him than his logic dictated. He would *not* allow her to confuse him any more than he already was.

And to that end, he decided to keep his broken engagement to Magda quiet for a while longer. Besides, Magda had her pride, too, and he had already promised that she could take credit for their estrangement.

He refused to think about Katherine using the information to further their own relationship. And friendship was all there was between them.

Taking a sip of his brandy, he tested the word in his mind. Friend. Yes, that was it.

His body finally began unwinding from the tight coil he'd felt earlier. But it wasn't until the middle of the night that his eyes closed and blocked out the view of the ceiling, which happened to be the floor of Katherine's bedroom.

"KATHERINE! Wake up!" Clay stood in the hall directly outside her door, knocking loudly enough to wake her and all his neighbors. He had bounded up the stairs, having overslept himself. One of his most important clients was due in the office early this morning. Now, here he stood in the hallway, a chocolate velour robe belted at his waist and no time to spare. "Damn," he muttered under his breath, reaching for the handle. Stopping just inside the room, he stared at the view in front of him.

At first glance Katherine looked like a lost child in the middle of the large bed. She was on her back, her head turned toward the window that bled dim light into the room. One hand was outstretched, her fingers lightly curled, while the other rested sweetly on her abdomen.

But a step closer dispelled that first impression. Her red hair spilled across the pillows like streaks of brilliant lightning in the dim room. Rumpled sheets were kicked down toward the bottom of the bed to drape her legs erotically. The skimpy, deep-blue teddy barely covered her; peeping from the top was one dusky red-gold nipple. The breath caught in his throat. The straps were almost invisible, showing more creamy skin than should be legal. That, combined with the plunging neckline proved that if he had thought her complexion was beautiful, it was only because he'd had nothing else to compare it with.

"Katherine, wake up. It's time to go to work." His voice sounded strained even to his own ears.

She turned her head toward him. "No," she said slowly and distinctly.

Anger and frustration filled him. "Dammit, wake up! I'm not your mother!"

Her eyes opened then, and Clay almost fell into the vulnerable, green pools. They stared at each other, heightening tension singing in the air between them. Again she smiled. "I'm sorry. I was dreaming and your voice fit right in."

He watched her sit up, pulling the sheet up to rest on her breasts. He couldn't move, couldn't breathe, and his hands were mangling the ties of his robe. "What were you dreaming?" he finally managed, his imagination going crazy with the possibilities.

"Nothing."

His brows rose. "Nothing? I was in your dream and you call it nothing?" he teased, trying to rid himself of the tension.

"It's none of your business." She pushed her hair back over her shoulder, then glared at him with eyes that were now wide open.

She obviously slept with her jewelry on. The earrings dangled conspicuously from her small lobes, catching the early-morning light and twinkling at him as if they were winking. He forced himself to look back in her eyes.

Suddenly the tension in his body eased. He had the upper hand and it felt great. "I think the least you could do is tell me about my part in your dream." He should have been prepared, but he wasn't.

Pulling away the covers, Katherine scrambled to her feet on the mattress, hands belligerently on her hips, tousled hair like a red halo around her face, her jade-green eyes spitting fire. "You're right. You ought to know what you were doing so that it won't happen in real life! I had been working late and when I walked into the living room, you were making mad passionate love to some big-bosomed woman on the carpet in front of the fireplace."

Her eyes narrowed. She obviously didn't have his complete attention. Well, she amended, she did, but not by her loud declaration.

His eyes were glued to her breasts. The small pearl buttons at the top of her teddy had come undone and exposed a smooth expanse of skin down to her navel. She sighed heavily, looking down at herself. "I know, it's terrible, isn't it? When God was giving out bosoms, I must have been reading a comic book."

"Get dressed," he ordered tightly. "We leave in half an hour."

Her mouth opened to answer him, but before the words came to mind he was out the door and halfway down the stairs. She wouldn't let the tears fall. If he thought her body was that ugly, he could damn well do without her words of apology!

But all morning the image of him standing over her bed haunted her. The soft brown robe emphasized his build and complemented his golden tan. His streaked hair hadn't been brushed yet and looked as if a wanton woman had trailed her nails through it while making love. Her fingers itched to do the same....

CLAY JERKED the water taps, setting the temperature as cold as he could stand. Damn her! She knew damn well she was beautiful! And her breasts! Small enough to fill his palm, they were perfectly proportioned for her tiny size! But it was the golden-red peek of a nipple that had disturbed him the most. It begged to be touched, caressed. Suckled.

He clenched his hands into fists, only to unclench them and wrestle with the knot of his robe. He slammed into the shower, praying that the cold water would shock his senses and wipe out the picture of her standing there, her breasts high enough for him to lean over and taste. He had been just inches away.

The soap turned to mush in his hand as he held it tightly, squeezing it between his fingers. Damn her hide! He made quick work of the icy shower, rinsing as fast as possible and stepping out to dry and rub the goose bumps away.

The man in the mirror stared back at him, and suddenly his shoulders slumped. "You're a stupid fool, Reynolds." But that wasn't new news. He'd known that ever since he had met Katherine O'Malley.

THEY HAD FINISHED dressing, quickly downed their coffee and driven in silence until Clay stopped at the first red light. He glanced at her, holding out his wallet. "Here. Take some money and buy some clothes."

"No, thank you." Her hands remained primly in her lap.

"Take it." He waved it in her direction again as the light changed and traffic flowed.

"I admit I'm a little unusual, Mr. Reynolds, but I'm not after your money."

"Look. I don't want to insult you, but what you're wearing isn't really suitable for the office. Buy a few skirts and blouses that will mix and match and I'll deduct it from your paycheck."

Her eyes were downcast. He was right about her clothing, and it didn't help that feeling of inadequacy she'd been fighting all morning. A frown marred her brow. "Are you open to a deal, Mr. Reynolds?"

His wary glance almost made her smile. "Is it harmful or illegal?"

Just for a second a smile teased her lips. "No. At least I don't think so. Will you loan me a thousand dollars for clothing and my enrollment fee for college? I have collateral."

"What?"

She reached into her purse and pulled out a small brown velvet bag. Spilling the contents into her palm, she held out her hand. "My earrings."

"Your mother's earrings," he corrected softly. "And if I remember correctly, they were your father's wedding gift to her."

"But they're mine now. To do with as I wish. Will you accept them in exchange for a thousand dollars?"

He pulled into his parking slot and killed the engine, then swiveled toward her. "No."

Her heart plummeted. She lowered her hand to her lap, her eyelids hiding the green depths of her eyes. His hand covered hers. "Katherine, I'll lend you the thousand—no strings attached. And you don't have to use your jewelry for collateral. They're yours and you shouldn't give away such a special heritage. Besides, they're antiques and worth much, much more than that."

"They were given to me to seek what I want. I need an education, Clay."

"I'll lend you the money," he repeated. "You don't need to hock your earrings."

She raised her head, her eyes sheened with tears. She swallowed hard. "Will you take them anyway? As a gift?"

"Katherine, I . . ."

"Please?"

Her green eyes were wide and round as she waited for his answer. She didn't realize he had no choice. "Yes," he said, holding out his hand.

Very carefully she placed the earrings in his care. A feeling of rightness with this decision flowed through her. He didn't know it but she had given them to him in love. He was the only person she would ever give them to. . . .

Clay gazed down at the sparkling jewels, amazed at the warmth they exuded. The deep green of the emerald was only as bright as the brilliance of the small diamonds that dangled on intricate gold threads. He stared at them, mesmerized.

"You won't regret it, Clay," she told him softly, breaking the spell the jewels seemed to have created.

"We'll see," he said cryptically, placing the earrings back into the velvet bag and stuffing it into his inside suit pocket. "I'll have Consuela cash a check for you."

"Oh, and Clay?"

"Hmm?"

"May I borrow one of the company cars today? I have to go to the mall on my lunch hour."

"Right. Yes. Of course."

"Good. I promise I won't be long."

"Do you have a driver's license?"

"Of course." She looked surprised. "I can even drive an eighteen-wheeler, although I admit the opportunity doesn't come up that often."

He grinned. He couldn't imagine any man letting an imp of a girl behind the wheel of all that metal.

As if she read his mind, she answered, "It takes strength, not length. Just because I'm not tall doesn't mean I can't do anything anyone else can do."

"Except reach tall shelves."

"Without a little help," she clarified, aware of the smile hiding in the corners of his mouth.

"Or change light bulbs."

"Without a little help," she repeated. "But there are several things I can do that taller people can't."

"Such as?"

"I can slide down a chimney."

"Like Santa Claus?"

She nodded vigorously. "I can also climb under beds and hide in cabinets. And I can fix Japanese cars."

His brow furrowed, losing her logic. "What does fixing Japanese cars have to do with being small?"

"The Japanese workers in the auto factories are all small with tiny hands, so their engines are built with enough space between the engine parts for hands the size of theirs. Mine are perfect."

She sounded so smug, he couldn't help the laughter that burst from his throat. Her logic was irrefutable even if it was a little strange. "I'll keep that in mind," he finally managed.

"You do that." She grinned, pleased that she could make him laugh after watching him frown all morning.

CLAY PROMISED himself all day that he would call Laura and ask her to take Katherine as a roomer, sweetening the pot a little by helping with the rent. Laura needed all the money she could get her hands on just to keep that newly acquired prehistoric house of hers standing. It seemed the right thing to do for both Laura and Katherine.

Katherine took a two-hour lunch break, and when she returned she was ecstatic. She'd not only bought a few items to wear at the office, she'd also picked up the summer schedule and enrollment forms for San Antonio College.

By the time the day was over, Clay still hadn't made that call. He would talk to Laura tomorrow, he promised himself, ignoring the fact that he could have found the time that afternoon if he had really wanted to.

He made one stop on the way home, to buy another alarm clock. There was no sense tempting the devil by waking Katherine himself in the morning.

They ate a quiet dinner and watched a new movie on TV, then Clay sat in the study and went over papers from the office.

But that night, lying in bed, he couldn't close his eyes and allow sleep to come. Katherine was just upstairs.

The rest of the week followed the pattern of that first day. They came home, took turns cleaning and cooking, then spent a quiet half hour together before he went to the study and Katherine picked up another book. Katherine, he discovered, was a voracious reader.

Tonight, after cooking a light meal, they were sipping wine and having a lively discussion on the office.

Deep down inside, not even quite put into words yet, was the knowledge that he had to move Katherine into Laura's by tomorrow. It had to be done, he knew that, and yet . . .

He tasted the wine from the fluted glass sitting next to him. "Are you enjoying your work? Is being a secretary everything you thought it would be?"

"I love it," she said simply. "And when I go home, there's never the smell of liver and onions on my hands and in my hair."

He remembered the night her scent had surrounded him like a heavenly fog as he had sat on the couch and felt her warmth in the cushions. Her hair hadn't smelled of anything but sweet wildflowers then. He chuckled aloud, if only to relieve the discomfort the memory evoked.

They talked about all sorts of things besides the office. And though he knew they were each keeping the bad parts of their lives from the other, that was okay, too. There was never a silence that wasn't relaxed, and never a conversation where one of them couldn't pick up the ball and run with it. It was amazing.

They wound up with Clay sitting on one end of the couch while Katherine was curled on the other, and continued talking until late in the night. He had refilled their glasses occasionally with the wine they had opened at dinner, but neither had had enough to be even slightly drunk.

It was the most relaxing evening Clay had ever spent. She was witty and warm and wonderful, and he found himself relating all kinds of things he never thought he would tell anyone. Her warm, husky laughter ran down his spine like chilled champagne as he regaled her with some of the episodes he and David and Laura had shared.

But when Katherine's beautiful green eyes were closing and they still hadn't moved toward their beds, he reluctantly held out his hand. "Come on, sleepyhead. It's time to go to bed."

"I know," she said, hiding a yawn. "It's been so nice I just hate to end the evening."

He chuckled. "I think the evening ended itself."

Placing her hand in his, she rose, only to wind up pressed against his body. His breath caught in his throat. Without thinking of the consequences he bent his head, his eyes focusing on her slightly parted lips.

He tried to hold back, he swore he did. But the instant his lips met hers, a craving deeper than his very soul cried out and he lost himself in her touch. His arms encircled her small waist, crushing her to him so he could feel all of her against every inch of his hard body.

His tongue stroked between her teeth, ravishing the inside of her mouth, stealing the softness for himself. His ears rang with the need for her. A groan echoed from deep in his throat, a sound that bared his warring frustration and need to the woman in his arms.

"I knew it would be this way," he growled when he finally broke the kiss. But he couldn't stand it. His mouth craved to touch and taste the rest of her flesh, the curl of her earlobe, the slim side of her neck. Her taste was nectar, her scent a field of mind-drugging poppies.

"Shhh," she whispered in his ear, her tongue riding its rim. "Again, Clay. Kiss me again." Her hands ran through his hair, her fingers teasing him with their butterfly touch.

His arms tightened even more as he claimed her mouth again. He was shaking with the need to have her, to be with her. Never, ever before had he felt so weak and so strong. Never had he craved a woman to the point of crying his needs aloud.

"Katherine," he muttered, his lips branding her eyes, her cheeks, her nose. "Katherine."

"Please, Clay," she whispered pleadingly, sprinkling kisses on his face and neck. She was so tiny, her head barely came to his chest. "Please."

Her mouth was level with his hard male nipple and her tongue shot out to dampen his shirt before suckling gently through the material. Another groan issued from his throat, and his shaking hand reached for her breast. He had been right. She fit perfectly into the palm of his hand, her nipple pressing against the center as if teasing him with her arousal. "Perfect. Dear Lord, it's just perfect," he muttered hoarsely.

"More," she whispered, bringing her mouth up to his. "I want more, Clay." Her hips swayed with his, her softness accommodating his hardness and almost sending him over the brink to ecstasy.

His hands fit against her buttocks, lifting her up and holding her pinned against him as he buried his mouth in the curve of her neck and inhaled deeply, trying to keep his mind from spinning dizzily out of control. He shouldn't be doing this. There was a reason, but for the life of him, he couldn't remember what it was. His senses were filled with her. No matter what he gave, she gave more, and he wanted it all.

"I promise," she choked, tears streaming down her face as she scattered heated kisses on his neck and chest. Her mouth felt like a white-hot branding iron, and he thought he would burst with the pleasure of it. "I won't ask for more. Just this once, Clay. Just once."

His hands tightened, then stilled. His breathing sounded loud and ragged in the quiet room. And he still couldn't let her go. Not yet.

He wrapped his arms around her and rested his head against the crown of her hair. Then he rocked back and forth, as if giving comfort to a baby. "Shhh, it'll be all right. Shhh," he kept saying, wondering who he was comforting, her or himself.

But he had to release her. He knew it. It hurt like hell to unwrap his arms from her softness, then take a step back from the one thing he craved most at the moment.

"Go to bed, Katherine."

"But . . ."

"I said, go to bed!" He turned toward the empty fireplace, unable to look at her eyes and see the pain reflected there.

As she reached down and picked up her shoes he slowly pivoted to watch, something inside him wanting to punish himself. With back rigid and head high, she swayed out of the room, never looking back. He couldn't take his eyes from her retreating form.

It took all night to calm down, but that was okay, because he had all night. Tomorrow he would call Laura and arrange things for Katherine. Then he would pray she would forgive him for losing control.

But he knew that this moment of insanity would cost him dearly. He couldn't hide from his own emotions anymore.

NOTHING WAS SAID the next morning. Not a word. And all day long Clay stayed out of Katherine's way. Consuela sent him looks that pointed to the fact he was acting unnaturally, but he didn't care. He was too busy lashing himself with his own whips of guilt to worry about his secretary adding to it.

At midmorning Consuela stepped inside his office with fresh coffee and coffee-cinnamon cookies. "What's this?" he snapped, not wanting the interruption, nor the advice that was dying to trip off Consuela's tongue.

"Spicy hermits," she snapped back, walking out of the room, her back ramrod straight.

By late afternoon he wasn't fit to talk to anyone. Except Laura. And when he called, he almost sounded natural. Almost. She agreed to see him right away.

He strode from the office toward the outside door. "Consuela, do you think you could drop Katherine at my place after work?"

"Your place? Sure."

"Good. I'll see you Monday, then."

He didn't look at Katherine, but all the way to the door he could feel her eyes on him, silently condemning him for his odd behavior. And she had every right in the world to do so.

LAURA LOOKED cool and beautiful, as usual. Clay put on his best, easygoing smile and ignored the cold lump of guilt crouching in the pit of his stomach. "You look terrific."

She looked him over carefully, and he knew she spotted the dark circles under his eyes. "And you, dear friend, look like something the cat wouldn't bother dragging in."

She led the way into the kitchen and served him iced tea, but he didn't hear a word she said until she mumbled something about her car's air conditioning. Nothing was registering.

He had prepared a speech to convince her of the rightness of his idea, but somehow the words were sticking in his throat. "Laura, I need a favor," he blurted out. His eyes darted around the room, noting for the first time how shabby the old house was. "And you need extra money."

She chuckled. "No joke. The wiring in this monstrosity just cost me several thousand. If I was sane, I would have moved into an apartment instead of buying a house with character to renovate. Character is costly."

"I have a proposition," he began, telling her a little of Katherine's background, pretending he had nothing but a cursory interest in the girl.

But Laura was smarter than that and smelled a story. Her gaze pinned him to his chair. "And just where does she fit into your life? Aren't you still engaged to Magda?"

"Magda has nothing to do with Katherine," he hedged, unwilling to admit his engagement was off in case Laura told Katherine. He wasn't ready for that. Not yet. He knew he was creating one hell of a mess, but he didn't know what else to do. "Katherine's just a kid who needs a break and I'm in a position to help her." *Or hurt her*, his mind echoed. He forced himself to go on. "She'll pay half your mortgage payment a month, with the first payment in advance."

Chuckling, Laura held up her hands. "I'll say yes before you change your mind!" she exclaimed, and relief washed over him like a tidal wave.

An hour later Clay strolled out her door feeling much better about the future. Katherine's future. While feeling so content, Clay fixed Laura's car air conditioner. All it needed was freon, and his fiddling with it delayed the trip home and the confrontation with Katherine. *A coward dies a thousand deaths.*

Wherever he turned, he saw her green eyes shining with tears, and yet he knew that Katherine leaving his home was the best thing for everyone, especially after last night. He was already committed to his choice. Now that Magda was out of the picture and he had taken care of Katherine as any good friend should, he could continue with his path in life as a single man. Be-

sides, he tried to tell himself, wasn't one woman much
the same as the other when the newness wore off? Quick
of tongue and even quicker of pocket.

Somehow the conviction he usually held wasn't there
anymore. It was being replaced by doubts, and doubts
brought on an even deeper sense of frustration.

6

KATHERINE STOOD in the kitchen, a cola in her hand as she stared out the large bay window. The woodland scene wasn't helping to calm her nerves. She listened to Clay's hollow footsteps as he made his way from the front door to the kitchen. She knew when he reached the doorway, but she couldn't turn around and confront him. Wherever he had disappeared to this afternoon, she didn't want to know about it. Somehow she knew that he was going to say something she didn't want to hear.

"Katherine." His voice was quiet but the echo reverberated in her ears. "I found a place for you to stay."

She cleared her throat to ease the lump that formed there. Her heart plummeted. "I can't stay here?" She would not cry. She would not!

His voice sounded as sad as her soul felt. "We both know that's impossible. A friend of mine, Laura Sheridan, has offered to let you stay with her until you decide what you want to do."

She chose a tree and stared at it, willing it to turn into a club so she could hammer Clay over the head with it. The man was impossible! Didn't he know love when he saw it standing in front of him? "Will I continue working at the office?"

"Yes, of course. Consuela would kill me if you quit." He tried to put a smile in his voice, but he couldn't quite manage it. The office without Katherine? Impossible.

"When am I leaving?"

He allowed his eyes to trail up and down her spine and back again. She was so tiny, so very defenseless. So terribly alive and vibrant. "As soon as possible."

"Now?" She spun around. Her shimmering green eyes were as wide as saucers and as vulnerable as a child's.

An imaginary fist hit his stomach with all the force of a boxer's thrust. She was so beautiful and untamed! And everything he hadn't wanted—until now! He shook his head. "Tomorrow morning."

Katherine placed her glass carefully on the table, her hand drifting away from it to arc in the air. "Is this it, Clay? Are you going to ignore what happened between us and go on with your engagement to Magda knowing you'll *never* have what we almost had last night?"

Her eyes were steady, her face tilted toward him as if asking calmly for an answer to an office problem. Frustration raged within him, but he stifled it. If he tried to reason out his feelings, he wouldn't like what he saw. Taking a deep breath, he answered her woodenly. "What happened last night never should have taken place. I apologize."

"The apology is *not* accepted." Her voice was so firm, he was stunned by the rejection. "You have just taken away a very precious moment for me. I'm not sorry for what happened last night. I'm not ashamed of it."

"I don't feel ashamed," he began, fumbling for the words to make her understand that he had taken advantage of her and felt worse for that.

"Yes, you do." She took a step closer. Then another step. And another. "You feel guilty because of Magda." She placed her hand on his chest, bare inches from his heart. "I know," she said quietly. "Because I do, too."

His voice was a bare whisper. His pumping heart had picked up speed. "Why? What happened wasn't your fault. It was mine."

"We share the blame. I don't know if Magda is really right for you or not. Only you can decide that. But I know that if you were in love with her, you wouldn't have reacted to me the way you did—the same way I reacted to you."

He covered her hand with his, the warmth of her skin igniting a fire within. "I'm not dead, Katherine. Just engaged."

"To a woman who *doesn't* light your fire."

"You don't know what you're talking about."

She smiled. Slowly and devastatingly she allowed her eyes to speak her thoughts before she did. "Your heart is hammering against my palm. Your eyes are telling me that you still desire me." Her head tilted. "Tell me you don't want to kiss me again."

A groan emerged from deep inside his chest as the defences he had built crumbled like dust against her onslaught. Need became everything. He swept her hand from his chest to his back and enfolded her in a clasp that was as possessive as it was erotic. His lips crushed hers, pressuring her to open her mouth and receive him.

Katherine's fingers slipped up his back and sought the solidness of his flesh. Her arms tightened as she opened her mouth and became the aggressor. She pulled him toward her, molding every intricate curve of her body to his.

He moaned again. A voracious force was building inside him and he tried to control it, but his mind was numbed to everything but the taste of her, the scent of her, the feel of her.

He pulled away, sprinkling kisses on her cheek and neck. "I want you. You know that."

"I know," she said, smoothing his hair. "And I want you."

He knew this wasn't right, but for the life of him he couldn't help himself and stop now. Everything fled in the face of having Katherine in his arms. In his bed. With a swift movement he scooped her up and carried her to his bedroom, not halting until she was lying in the middle of his bed.

Sanity returned for just one moment, then Katherine's hands were busy pulling at his tie and he was lost again in the green depths of her eyes and the promise of fulfillment with the woman he wanted above all else. Soon she'd be gone and he wouldn't be able to touch her like this, watch her smile so sensuously or half close her eyes as if ecstasy were claiming her just because he was near.

His breath was warm and shallow, his touch as exciting as lightning. Katherine watched him reach out to caress her as if she were priceless. She ached for him, craved him so badly nothing else mattered. All those sleepless nights fantasizing about what it would be like to be with him were now being realized—and it was better than she had dreamed.

"You're so very special," she murmured, kissing his bared chest.

"Sweet heaven, so are you." He slipped the dress over her head and let it fall to the floor. All that covered her was a slim pair of black panties that left little to the imagination. "You're beautiful," he whispered, drifting one finger over her creamy bare breasts. "So tiny yet so perfect...."

His touch ignited a fire in the pit of her stomach and she stopped breathing, willing his touch to continue.

Her hand covered his cheek, and her eyes tried to tell him what her words could not. She wanted to ask him about his cryptic statement. Another time. Another time. *Now* was too precious to lose with conversation.

"You're so perfect, Katherine. So very perfect." Then his mouth tenderly claimed hers. She knew that they were both lost. Their bodies blending together wasn't enough; it would never be enough for her, but it had to do for now.

Tenderness turned to need and need to urgency. By the time Clay was undressed and sprawled next to her she didn't know anything but the sensual demands of her body. He was as essential as breathing. His caresses were intimate, coaxing, claiming. She could hardly speak with the need that he built inside her. "Clay, please," she finally pleaded against his shoulder, smelling the heady masculine scent of him as he teased her unmercifully.

She followed her verbal invitation by opening to him like a flower. But just before the first plunge, Clay stopped, poised above her. "Do you want me, Katherine? As much as I want you? Do you?" He teased her with his movements, and she felt the craving building into shooting sparks. "Tell me!"

"Yes. Yes!" she cried and his lips captured the sound as he plunged inside her, sending showers of light flowing through her body. Shimmering liquid waves of warmth poured over her, through her, surrounded her. She wanted to cry with the beauty of it.

Desire etched his expression as he rocked her body to an ageless rhythm. He thrust once more, and she was sure his spirit melded with hers, floating, entwined.

From far away she heard Clay call her name and her arms tightened in response, unwilling to relinquish her hold. She never wanted to be free of him. His weight felt secure and warm. His skin was heated, slick with exertion. His quickened breathing in her ear was the most wondrous music in the world.

Loving Clay was even more wonderful than she had thought it would be.

A deep sense of completion filled her every pore. But her smile disappeared. She sensed his withdrawal even before he pulled away. Silently she prayed that he wouldn't leave her, but something in the back of her mind resigned her to that fact.

But instead of reality intruding upon her idyll, he rolled to his side and pulled her with him until she was lying on top of him. He kissed the tip of her nose. "I don't know what to say, little one."

She smiled. "Tell me something positive."

His smile mirrored hers, but there was a sadness in his eyes. He gently pushed back a tendril of hair, curling it around her ear. "You're wonderful. I've never felt that way before. I'm stunned."

"Care to try for a repeat?"

His golden eyes opened wide, first in shock, then in need. He swelled against her immediately. Apparently his libido was more powerful than his thoughts.

"Yes," he growled, winding her hair in his hand and pulling her face down to his.

His kiss wiped out everything in her mind but him, including the consequences of the past hour. But she knew. Soon the piper would call for his tithe, and she'd be left in the cold. It would be silly to think that these past moments would change the course of their relationship. Had she not purposely seduced him? She didn't want to admit it, but already she was readying herself for the next blow.

The rest of the night was a dream. They made love, slept, made love again. His hunger was deep and his

need unquenchable. And each time they came together she knew that the morning would bring the
shock of parting.

She knew him well enough to realize that he would
still carry through his plans.

And she wasn't wrong.

The following morning he stood in the kitchen, a
hard, distant expression on his face.

"We're still going ahead as planned?"

"Yes."

"You're blind, Clay."

"Maybe. Maybe we both need the distance to decide
what should be done next."

"Scared of me?" she taunted, not allowing her heart
to release the tears that wanted to spill forth like a river.

"Yes."

His honesty surprised her. So did her own frustrated
anger. Her hands clenched. "Are you really so blind?
I'd make a better wife for you than Magda ever could.
I can't believe you're willing to throw it away."

"Katherine, I—"

She ignored his protest. "But you, rigid as you are,
are going to pass me by because I don't have the qual-
ifications you've decided you require in your spouse."
His brown eyes widened, and she nodded her head.
"Oh, yes, I figured it out. Little ol' me, with my G.E.D.
education, finally understood. You think you need
someone who moves in the 'right' circles and has the
right education—the right friends. Someone who will
let you walk all over her as you lead your own life. You
don't want a wife—you want a beautiful, handcrafted
doormat!"

She came so close that her body brushed his and her
scent filled his nostrils. She tapped her finger lightly
against his chest. "*You* are a coward, Clay Reynolds. I

don't understand why I love you at all. But I do. I only hope you come to your senses before it's too late." She reached on tiptoes and placed an airy soft kiss on his open mouth, then stepped around him, heading for her room and the suitcase she had to pack.

He wasn't following her, which was a blessing. She didn't think she could have kept her tears at bay much longer. It was with wooden movements that she succeeded in packing and walking back downstairs.

The scene in the car was another matter. She had had time to pull herself together. But so had Clay.

"You'll be happy at Laura's. She's a lovely lady."

Was the man dense, or what? "I'll be as happy with her as you'll be with Magda?" Katherine asked sweetly, but her voice was laced with arsenic.

"Cut it out," he gritted.

"You're a fool, Clay Reynolds."

"I won't argue."

There was nothing she could answer to that. Looking down at her plain black skirt and white blouse, she had to realize the truth. Aside from the guilt that weighed heavily on her shoulders for taking an engaged man to her bed and offering more than her heart, she should have seen their relationship from Clay's point of view. Magda came from the same social set as Clay. Maybe he was right. Magda suited him—and Katherine didn't.

Clay heaved a sigh. "Look," he began. "I have a business appointment today, but how about attending a concert with me tonight? As a friend? I have box seat tickets. Somebody ought to get some culture out of it."

She knew she should say no. She should shake him so hard his brains would fall out . . . "I'd love to. What's playing?"

"Ravel."

She wished she knew what that was. Instead, she said a very knowledgeable, "Oh." But her heart spun a thread of hope to hang on to.

EVEN IN HER MISERY, Katherine liked Laura as soon as she met her. Though Laura seemed preoccupied, that was just as well because so was Katherine.

In fact, ever since Katherine had been shown to her room, she'd been crying. Clay hadn't stayed in the house three minutes. He probably couldn't wait until she was out of his home and he could have his privacy and his life back. Damn him!

The tears started again. Was this hated, wonderful, star-studded, hell-ridden emotion called love *only* felt by her? Didn't Clay feel anything other than a normal sexual drive? While she knew a man didn't have to *like* a woman in order to *lust* after her body, she hadn't thought Clay was that way. He didn't seem to have a line of patter that he fed to a woman as if he were fishing for bass. Nor had he given her those purposely sexy, suggestive looks that were meant to be a come-on.

She sat up, wrapping her arms around her slim body. But his kiss! That kiss and lovemaking had been made up of spun-sugar clouds, and his eyes had lit with emotions that made her heart sing in response. He *had* to have felt something! All she could do was wait and let him realize just how much they had in common: love and needs and wants.

THE EVENING finally came. Until then, the minutes had been hours, the hours, days.

Katherine wore her best outfit, one she'd bought two years ago for a range dance. It was dark blue shot with pink as pale as an ocean sunset. The neck was high, the skirt draped. She had washed and tamed her hair with a dryer and brush, and it lay in seductive waves and curls on her shoulders. Never one to use much make-up, she didn't have any to use now.

A turn in the full-length mirror in her room confirmed what she already knew. She just wasn't sophisticated enough, beautiful enough, tall enough, to make anyone's heart beat faster. Cute as a button, as some of the truckers used to say, but certainly not a femme fatale.

She thought of pleading a headache, but the selfish part of her wanted to see him too badly to let this opportunity pass. Besides, she had promised Laura she would be out of the house for Laura's at-home dinner date with David. There was nothing she could do—except answer the doorbell.

Clay looked wonderful in a lightweight brown suit that pointed up his golden coloring, sun-kissed hair and beautiful brown eyes.

"Are you ready?" he asked, his voice almost a whisper. Her answering smile gave him his dose of vitamin C for the entire week. He hadn't seen her all day and in that time he'd forgotten just how beautiful she was. Heat unfurled in the pit of his stomach as his legs turned to cement. It dawned on him that making this date was probably his greatest mistake with Katherine yet. Last night was bad enough, but this was tempting fate.

Her words still echoed in his head. *I don't understand why I love you at all, but I do.* Those words were the most frightening words in the English language. He had always steered so far away from that particular emotion. It was synonymous with manipulation....

It was with concerted effort that he led her to the car, then got behind the wheel. Stupid! He had been stupid to see her again! After dropping her at Laura's he had returned home to sit and stare at the empty air for over an hour—all the time clutching the pair of antique earrings that held a fascination as strong as their owner did. Her spirit was everywhere. But her voice was gone. That lilting, wonderful, funny, sexy voice.

He'd spent half the afternoon attempting to explain his feelings to David. It was preferable to being alone in his own home, though he knew he'd get used to it. He'd concluded that their relationship would never have lasted the long haul; he and Katherine didn't have enough in common to help them over the many bumps that all relationships had to endure. Good sex wasn't enough.

Then why had he invited her to this concert? He should have left well enough alone.

As they arrived, the lights were dimmed and the orchestra was warming up. A murmur of voices could still be heard, like the droning of bees around a hive. Then came the tap of the conductor's baton on the podium and the crowd hushed.

The orchestra played their best that night, Clay was sure. Katherine sat straight-backed in her seat, a light flush of excitement tinting her cheeks. He watched her surreptitiously, thinking she was delightful. Although he hadn't asked her, he was sure this was her first concert and was glad that he was the one to introduce her to fine music. He would love to be the first to introduce her to a lot of things. . . . He shut down those thoughts that had sprung up on their own.

But his body didn't get the message. He shifted in his seat, relaxation replaced by irritation. Dammit! She shouldn't be able to do this to him! He should think of her as a little sister. He sighed resignedly. That didn't work, either.

When intermission was announced by the lights going on, Katherine blinked as if coming out of a trance. She turned toward Clay, her eyes filled with wonder. "How long is intermission?"

He smiled indulgently. "Only about twenty minutes. Care for a glass of champagne to while away the time?"

Her tongue darted out to rest on the peak of her upper lip. His eyes followed the movement, then without conscious thought, he imitated the act. "Last time I had champagne was at my brother's wedding and after one glass I told his new wife what I thought of her."

"How old were you then?"

"Seventeen."

"And now?"

"Twenty-six." She smiled, her green eyes merrily dancing with mischievous light. "And my brother's wife isn't here."

"Let's go."

He'd never been one for champagne, but he ordered two glasses anyway. They were standing by the side of the bar as Katherine attempted an explanation of the effect the music had on her when Clay's name carried across the lobby.

"Damn, man, fancy meetin' you here!" A large man with even larger hands patted Clay on the back.

Clay stuck out his hand for a vigorous shake. "Jim, I seem to be running into you everywhere I go," he said before making introductions. Mrs. Butler stood by her husband's side, quiet and, to Katherine, looking slightly cowed.

"You also seem to have a different girl with you every time I see you." The large man's eyes narrowed on Katherine, practically undressing her. "My, my, what a pretty little girl."

"Lady," she corrected, looking him straight in the eye.

His brows rose and a rumble erupted from his chest. "Fiesty little thing, isn't she?"

"Lady," she said again, a smile slightly defusing her correction. "I am a female over the age of consent, Mr. Butler. Don't let my size fool you."

"You sure got that right, little one. You're all female, all right." His appreciative gaze began undressing her again, and Clay felt newborn antagonism welling in his chest.

But before he could say a word, Katherine spoke up. "I also have a brain. Female variety. It tells me that if you're not kind to little ladies, you're also not kind to your wife or your dog."

"Well, damn!" he said, attempting a grin but not pulling it off. "Some women don't know a compliment when they hear one."

Katherine gave him a piercing look, then set her empty champagne glass on the edge of the bar. "Excuse me, Mr. Reynolds," she said quietly. "I'll be in my seat when the music begins."

Stunned, Clay watched her walk across the lobby to the door marked Ladies and disappear. He wasn't sure who he was more furious with, Jim Butler for his obnoxious behavior or himself for wanting it to pass. A flash of pride seared through him even as he tried to think of something that would placate his business associate.

"Whew, that little lady's in a twitch. Is she one of them women's libbers? I don't like them too much. Not too much at all."

Once more Clay began to answer, but this time Mrs. Butler beat him to it. "That's obvious, Jim. On top of everything else, don't be so blasted obvious!" The older woman stalked off toward the same door that had swallowed Katherine.

Jim stood next to Clay, muttering as he watched his wife enter the ladies' room. He had no style but he wasn't a bad man, Clay knew, just totally ignorant of human emotions. If it wasn't in black and white, Jim couldn't see it. Clay had worked with him for years and had found him to be scrupulously fair. But he came from the old school of Texans: the one which held there was nothing like a man and nothing better than a Texas man. In Jim Butler's book that placed women as third-class citizens.

The older man had looked at Magda the same way, but Clay hadn't found himself swamped by this feeling of overwhelming protectiveness then. He tried to justify his feelings and his first thought was that he wanted to protect her because she had made herself vulnerable to him by admitting she loved him. That didn't hold water.

Deep down inside he knew it was time to search for some answers, and he had a feeling that he wasn't going to be too pleased with a few of them.

The rest of the evening was a disaster. Katherine came back to the box and sat next to him as the lights dimmed. Her back was stiff and she looked as if her facial muscles had frozen just as she was eating a lemon. Even at that she was darling.

It wasn't until they were pulling up to the front of Laura's house that Katherine spoke to him again. "That's the most obnoxious man I've ever met. Even some of the truckers know better than to approach a woman that way!"

"You didn't handle that whole episode very well, either," he stated quietly. "You purposely tried to provoke him."

Her eyes were large green pools as she turned to him. "You're right. I don't suffer fools in silence, Clay. I never have and I won't start now. At least I'm honest about it."

He ran a hand through his hair. "Sometimes I think honesty is another word for lack of tact. It allows people to voice all kinds of opinions that shouldn't be spoken aloud."

"That hurts." Her words were so simple, so direct.

"Katherine," he began, but her fingers came up to rest on his lips.

"Since we're talking honestly, listen to me a moment. Don't say anything, just listen." He nodded, afraid she would remove her hand and he would lose the warmth of her fingers playing across his mouth. The feeling spread through his body as his eyes followed the nuances of her expression.

"I love you, Clay Reynolds. I'm not supposed to, but I do. I know I wouldn't really make as good a wife for you as Magda could. I'd be possessive of your time, I wouldn't fit in with your friends and business associates and I'd probably say the wrong things at the wrong times, like I did tonight. I'm not dumb, I'm just not as tactful as she probably is. But I'm willing to learn anything you think I need to know. In return, I can give you more love than you ever dreamed of holding. I can give you children and a home that sings with happiness. I can give you all that and more."

"Don't," he protested, his voice hoarse. But before he could speak again she whisked her hand away replacing it with her lips. His world tilted as she sought the inner recesses of his mouth the way he had done to her just nights before. Her hands rested on both sides of his clean-shaven face, touching him as if he were a gift she must return but would relish until then.

As he sought to pull her close, she leaned away. "Not yet. You don't see it yet, Clay. But I'm hoping you will.

Soon." She traced the line round his mouth with a fingernail. "Honesty isn't a bad word, really. It's the most important word in the English language—especially when you're talking to yourself." She gave him another fleeting kiss, her lips as soft as butterfly wings. "Good night. Sleep tight."

Then she was out of the car and running up the walk toward the darkened house, swallowed by the night.

He had a lump in his throat from a declaration he knew came straight from her heart. There was also his own answering declaration that he couldn't put into words. He wasn't sure what love was, and didn't know how to explain himself or his emotions half as eloquently as she did.

"Sleep tight." Those magic words again. He had a fleeting image of her leaning over a crib and saying those same words to a baby, a baby with golden-red hair and big green eyes and a smile that could line the sky with rainbows.

TEARS CASCADED down Katherine's cheeks as she closed the door. She shouldn't have said anything to Clay. He was still attempting to sort out his emotions, look at them logically and deduce an answer. That was fine for a business problem, but it didn't work with personal relationships at all.

She walked into the kitchen, pushing against the swinging door to find the lights on and Laura nursing a cup of hot tea. If it was possible, Laura looked worse than Katherine did. "What's wrong?" Laura said with a sniffle.

What was the sense of pretending, thought Katherine? "I'm miserable. Miserable and frustrated and ready for a fight."

Before Katherine knew it, they were both laughing through their tears. She explained how she felt, but somehow the words weren't as true as when she was sitting in the car next to Clay.

Laura sighed. "What a pair we make. I want David, but in order to get his full attention I'll have to pursue him as if I were a renegade cop after a killer. I'm just not that open. I can't even get him to become a friend, while you've gotten to friendship and can't get to the next step."

"Your date didn't work out, either," Katherine commiserated.

Shrugging, Laura said morosely, "It did for a while. Then, after a kiss that could have set the carpet on fire, he slammed out the door!"

"Same thing here. Only I slammed through the door, instead."

"So far we're not doing too well," Laura said. "I'm just about ready to give up. David will just have to find another best friend and lover—apparently he's not willing to let me fill that role."

Best friends and lovers were Katherine's specialty. She'd seen enough of both at the truck stop. Transient men and even more transient women, long weekends and then on the road again until the next time. It was unusual when there wasn't a woman in the café crying on a Monday over a guy she'd met on Friday.

"We just need to pool our resources, that's all. If you teach me how to be a lady, I'll teach you how to loosen up," Katherine offered, wondering if either was possible. On the other hand, what did she have to lose?

They began immediately, staying up until dawn as they rummaged through magazines, filling scratch pads with crude drawings of dresses and hairstyles and writing lists of things that each needed to explain to the other.

"I'll show you how to set a full table tomorrow. There are a minimum of three forks, three spoons and two knives, and they all have to be in a certain spot. We'll work on the glasses and plates later." Laura yawned.

"Right. Later," Katherine mumbled, her head nodding with exhaustion. "See you then."

Sunday was the same. Each went over everything the other seemed to think important, including walking properly and laughing discreetly.

"I thought all you had to do was get from one side of the room to the other and you were in business." Katherine dropped the book from her head for the hundredth time.

"Wrong. It has to be a glide, as if you're on skates. And the less anatomy that wiggles, the better."

Katherine was honestly glad to see the sun rise on Monday morning. At least she could forget the table-setting procedures emblazoned on the backs of her eyelids! And she had thought that eating peas with a fork instead of a spoon was a step up in the world!

Laura called the office in late afternoon. "Katherine, is Clay very busy?"

"No, but he's like an armadillo without his shell, scurrying into any available hole so he won't have to see me," she declared, angry that she hadn't been able to corner him yet and find out what his reaction to her speech was. On second thought, maybe this *was* his reaction!

Laura's chuckle carried over the line. "Don't worry. Knowing Clay, it's going to get worse before it gets better."

Katherine sighed, running a hand around her neck to ease the tension there. "Thanks for the encouragement. So far he's not too impressed with the new me. But I went shopping at lunch and bought a few new outfits like the ones we discussed. Maybe he'll notice tomorrow."

"I bet he's already noticed," Laura surmised with a chuckle. "If he's gone into hiding then he's already recognized a difference and just doesn't know how to cope with it yet. Clay's a man of habit. He has to think of things a long time before he's ready to accept them."

"Is a century too long to wait?" Katherine asked dryly, earning another chuckle.

"It'll be sooner than that. Oh, by the way, I may not be home tonight. Don't worry about me if I don't show up, okay?"

"David?"

"David," she confirmed.

"Bingo. Good luck!"

"Thanks. Same to you and Clay."

"Fat chance," Katherine muttered, putting Laura through to Clay. Why couldn't she think of any really *good* Irish curses when she needed them? She knew there was one for practically every occasion, but she wanted one to fit Clay's hardheadedness.

Consuela dropped her off at Laura's later that day. Katherine couldn't help grinning as she remembered the note she had left on Clay's desk just before leaving. He had been in the men's room—again.

Mr. Reynolds

Would you please pick me up for work tomorrow? Laura has plans with David and I have no transportation until my next paycheck.

Thank you.

She had a small surprise for him when he came to get

her, one that would remind him she was definitely a grown-up woman.

NOT BOTHERING to turn on the lights, Clay slipped off his jacket and threw it on the couch, following it with his shirt and socks. His shoes were just inside the door. With tired movements he walked across the room to the bar and poured himself a stiff drink. Then, like a magnet drawn to the source, he walked back to the spot where Katherine used to stand. Sipping the biting liquid, he stared out into the dark night.

Finally his eyes had been pried open to show him that he had made one right decision in this past two weeks of chaos. He'd seen how really lonely he was—a loneliness that Magda wouldn't have been able to assuage no matter how hard she tried.

Magda as a beautiful and charming woman was incomparable. Magda as his wife and the mother of his children, sharing a private day-to-day life, spelled boredom. Lots of it.

He hadn't realized it before. He'd been so damn busy with his *own* list of requirements in a woman that he'd been boring, too.

At breakfast, memories of a red-haired sprite had overwhelmed him. He recalled how she'd told stories about herself and about life in a truck stop until she had him chuckling all the way to the office. In fact, he didn't remember ever enjoying himself more. He'd also learned a lot about Katherine through her anecdotes. All he had to do was read between the lines. Their conversations had taught him all about life—and surviving to live and learn another day.

But making one mistake didn't mean he had to make two. Katherine wasn't the automatic choice for a wife simply because Magda was the wrong woman for him.

Katherine was fun and witty, but most of the time she was out of his control. She was the most frustrating woman he had ever laid eyes on. And the good old-fashioned lust he felt for her wasn't the answer to boredom. She *made* more complications than she cured.

He ran a hand around his neck, attempting to ease the tension from his stiff muscles. For a man who'd never had woman problems before, he sure as hell had his hands full now! It had been three weeks since he'd met Katherine, and he hadn't slept a wink since.

He padded to the couch and went through his coat pocket. Inside, in a scrawled hand that he was beginning to know as well as his own, was a note from Katherine asking him to pick her up in the morning.

Clutching it in one hand, he walked into the bedroom and opened the nightstand drawer. Glittering on top of the chocolate-colored velvet bag lay her antique emerald and diamond earrings. Somehow they had woven their own spell on him. He held them in his hand, no longer amazed at the warmth they exuded. With a heavy sigh he lay down on top of the spread. Amazingly, within seconds, he was asleep, a smile on his lips, the earrings still in his hands.

7

THE NEXT MORNING he was late. He should have known that once he was finally able to ease Katherine from his mind and find sleep, he'd overdo it.

But she was his first waking thought in the morning, and he was as excited about seeing Katherine as he was reluctant. Her declaration of love, along with his constant need to take her in his arms and make mad passionate love to her one more time, warred with his fear of allowing himself to get emotionally involved. Emotions had never entered his previous relationships, and this was a completely new set of circumstances for him. He'd never felt this way before: wanting to run from a woman as much as he wanted to run *to* her, and he didn't know what to do. Katherine's presence in his life kept him in a constant state of turmoil.

Not seeing Laura's car in the driveway made him wonder how things were going with his friends. Maybe David had finally talked Laura into having the grand affair he had craved from her for so long. Clay hoped so, for both their sakes.

But all those thoughts of goodwill for his friends fled his mind as Katherine opened the door. In fact, he didn't have a thought left to ponder.

Katherine stood in the shadowed hallway, a black, filmy teddy hugging her tiny, perfect figure, leaving just enough to the imagination to be deadly. Even in the heat of the morning, he could see her nipples pushing against the silky fabric, and his breath stopped. Her hair was a riot of soft red curls framing her beautiful face. He swallowed hard, unable to think of a thing to say.

Her long, slim legs were encased in black hose attached to sexy black lace garters that seductively peeked from the hem of her teddy. Tall high heels of the same color graced her feet.

"I'm sorry I'm running late. Could you give me just a moment?" she asked softy, her tone low and seductive, her inflection not hurried at all.

Then he noticed the makeup, a flawless job on already flawless skin. "What the hell . . . !"

"Please. Just step inside. I'm almost through ironing my dress."

And, like the idiot he was, he did. "Was this planned?" he finally demanded, ignoring the fact that his body responded instantly to the woman in front of him. His mind might be failing, but all his other parts were in excellent working order.

She turned smartly and headed for the kitchen. "Coffee? And yes."

He followed, his eyes never leaving her swaying derriere, until her answer registered. Then he stopped in the kitchen doorway.

"Yes?"

She picked up the iron, daintily stuck out her tongue and licked her finger. With a flick of her wrist, she tested the heat of the iron. It sizzled. So did he. "Yes."

He didn't know how to respond to her honesty, but his body knew what to do. He restrained himself. Barely. Most women weren't fond of the idea of being thrown down on a kitchen floor and ravished by a half-crazed maniac.

He muttered the only word that came to his deranged mind. "Mud flaps." The tinkle of her laughter sent shafts of delightful pain through him to rest heavily in the pit of his stomach—and elsewhere.

He cleared his throat. "Why?"

"When I realized I was running late, I decided welcoming you dressed this way was infinitely better than greeting you naked as the day I was born." She began ironing the skirt of the dress stretched on the board.

"Infinitely," he repeated, pouring himself a cup of coffee and trying in vain to keep his eyes to himself. Suddenly he slammed his cup down on the counter and turned, reached for her arm in frustration. "Do you dress this way when David comes over?" he demanded.

She smiled. A secret smile. "No."

"No?"

Her lips puckered before the soft, slow sound flowed out. "No."

He jerkily turned back to his coffee. Tension seized his body. He was aware of his need, having suffered from it several times before, but never this strongly, this persistently. This hotly. It was as if all the summer day's heat was pouring through him at once, curling around his limbs in anticipation of intense pleasure. Before, he had always taken his pleasures and moved on to another heat, another summer, another woman.

But this woman was different. Instead of the heat lessening, it worsened, crippling him with the force of it. Her lips were parted and slightly pouty, and he wanted to taste them. Her curves tempted his hands to seek them. Her perfume filled his nostrils and senses, making him heady with the scent. And still—stubbornly—he refused himself her pleasure, for her sake even more than his.

She was too vulnerable. He didn't want her to be hurt when boredom set in and the time came for him to walk away. And having an affair, even a long one, wasn't suited to her emotional makeup. She wasn't prepared for the free-and-easy life-style some women enjoyed today. She was the kind who wanted marriage and kids and a backyard swing. He wasn't ready for that.

But the powerful emotions Katherine forced from him also scared the hell out of him. They were more potent than anything he had experienced before, stronger than he had ever imagined could be possible. He could feel his aching response to her nearness in every pore of his body.

The only thing he had that she could share was his money. Most women he knew wanted that almost as much as he did.

Come to think of it, he wasn't sure what he wanted anymore. Dammit! Katherine represented everything foreign to him, and foreign meant frightening.

"Clay?" Katherine's voice broke into his thoughts and he turned, only to stand, stunned. She was beautiful.

Her black cotton sheath was high-necked, cap-sleeved and demure—and probably the sexiest thing he had ever seen. She held her hair up like a curtain and turned, inviting him to a view of her exposed back. "Could you do the zipper for me? I can't reach."

His hands shook as he grasped the pull tab and brought it up. His knuckles grazed the softness of her neck and he almost groaned with the effort of pulling his hand back. He took a deep breath, commanding his body to do his will.

Katherine turned and smiled, looking serene, confident and just a little mysterious. "Ready?" she asked brightly.

He cleared his throat. "We're flying to Dallas for the day," he announced, amazed at his words and wondering where on earth that decision had come from. He did have an appointment there, but until the moment he'd just spoken, he hadn't known he was taking Katherine along.

"Today?"

"Yes." His voice was curt, but he was lucky he had a voice at all. "I have a business deal to complete and need you along to take notes."

"My shorthand is almost nonexistent," she warned, but her green eyes were alight with excitement. He took credit for that, enjoying her enjoyment.

"It'll do," he muttered gruffly, ushering her out the door, his hand on her arm. "We'll be back before dinner."

"Okay." She smiled, and his heart expanded to fill his whole body.

Without allowing himself to dwell on his decision or to let his gaze linger on her, he drove directly to the airport, gaining entrance to the section where the private planes were kept. Nodding to the man at the gate, he gunned the powerful car engine and traveled down the row of hangars until he pulled in front of his. A small green-and-white plane was being checked over by two workmen in overalls.

"Is it yours?" Katherine asked, her voice so low he could hardly hear.

"Yes." He flipped off the ignition and pocketed the keys. "It's a Bonanza F33A," he said proudly, knowing she probably knew nothing of planes, but having to identify his pride and joy anyway.

She shook her head, slipping out of the car seat and walking slowly toward the plane.

He watched her, mesmerized. When he realized the mechanics were looking at him, he shook his head to rid himself of the spell and walked into the hangar. Before his mind deserted him completely, he had to call Consuela and tell her of his plans to take Katherine.

FIFTEEN MINUTES LATER they were in the air.

"Are you all right?" he asked, leveling the plane and heading for Dallas's Love Field.

"Wonderful! I think I'm in love with flying!" She leaned back in the plush seat and gave a big sigh.

"Is this your first flight?"

"Yes! Isn't this great? Have you flown long? When did you get your first plane? How did you ever learn?"

He gave a deep chuckle, suddenly feeling freer than he had in weeks. Months. Years. "I've been flying since I was twenty-two, when a guy I knew took me up in his plane. I immediately signed up for lessons and I've been flying ever since. I love it, too."

"If I knew how to fly I doubt if I'd ever come out of the clouds," she answered, her eyes glued to the outside window.

He laughed again as he put the plane on automatic pilot. "Clouds are the very things a good pilot stays away from. There's turbulence in there."

"Really?" She stared at him with wide eyes, and he couldn't keep from looking at her. "When I was growing up I used to sneak up to the rooftop of our apartment over the truck stop and stare at the clouds, making imaginary animals out of them. Then I'd string together a story and hide in the make-believe world I had created."

"I can see you doing that," he murmured, his hand stretching out to touch the silk of her throat.

"What did you do when you were growing up?"

His eyes grew distant with the memory. "My escape was action. I skateboarded. I lived it, ate it, slept dreaming about it."

"You mean those things that look like scooters without handles?"

He grinned. "Those things," he said, "were my life. I thought I'd be world champion someday."

She tilted her head and stared at him. "And were you?"

"Alas, no. But I now own a skateboard park for kids, although it hardly breaks even, with the high insurance rates."

"Then why keep it?"

His face lost its smile as the edge of determination etched his jaw. "Because every kid needs a place to go and dream of making it big, while they're working off all that excess energy they don't know what to do with."

"You're a nice man, Clay Reynolds," she murmured softly. "Outside you're all rough, like lumpy papier-mâché and inside you're all soft, like marshmallows."

He frowned. "Hardly."

Katherine didn't answer. She just raised her brows as a small knowing smile tugged at the corners of her mouth.

ALMOST TWO HOURS later they landed at Love Field. Clay checked with the ground crew, then slipped Katherine inside the limousine that stood waiting for them. Katherine didn't say a word, but she touched everything from the rich velour upholstery to the buttons on the stereo and the small bottles hidden in the built-in bar.

Clay sat back and watched, enjoying her exploration. It was as if he was experiencing luxury for the first time, the excitement born again. He'd almost forgotten how many perks came with success....

"We're going to a strip shopping center?" Katherine whispered as the driver pulled in front of a small restaurant.

"Yes." He led her toward the brilliant, aqua-colored door. "But wait until you see what's inside," he promised as he led her into the cool, dark depths of one of Dallas's finest bistros. He refused to dwell on the fact that he'd never looked forward to a business lunch as much as this one.

They weren't alone again until Clay was once more piloting the plane back to San Antonio.

He listened to Katherine's remarks about his new client with surprise. She had far more insight into people and their behavior than he'd given her credit for. The owner had had a slight heart problem and wanted to relieve some of his stress. He wasn't averse to selling the strip, but was reluctant to sell the restaurant, which was his real love. Clay felt he could keep the previous owner on as manager of the restaurant and be better off for doing so.

Katherine concurred with his opinion, and he felt good. "And how are you enjoying working with Consuela?" he asked, remembering his conversation with the woman who had almost become his mother over the years.

"I love it. She's a very special lady, even though she sometimes intimidates me."

"Why does she intimidate you?"

"Because she knows so much, and I'm just learning."

"You'll catch on," he assured her, wondering what would happen to Katherine then. His gut tightened.

She grinned, and he tried to grin back. It didn't work. "Consuela is putting me on the computer tomorrow so I can learn more about the real-estate properties," she confided as he began their descent.

"Really? Why?"

"She thought I should know all aspects of the business if I'm going to be working for the office. It would help familiarize me with the entire operation."

"Remember just to observe. Let the salesmen handle the sales. They know what they're doing."

"Right, boss," she teased, only he couldn't crack a smile. He suddenly remembered that three of the salesmen were young, virile and single. . . .

Holding on to a distance he didn't feel, Clay dropped her back at Laura's and drove home, thankful there weren't any meetings to attend.

Morosely he sat in the living room while the sunset put on a spectacular show outside his window. He held Katherine's earrings in his hand, as mesmerized by the twinkling jewels as he was by their real owner. It was strange, but holding her earrings he felt connected to her in some way. He couldn't explain it—he just felt it.

When the doorbell rang, he was irritated at the intrusion until he discovered it was David on his porch.

"Hi! Need some company?" David asked, displaying a six-pack and a rather shaky smile.

"Why not?" Clay muttered, taking the offered beer and stalking back to plop down on the couch. He popped the top of a can. "How'd your date with Laura go?"

"Terrible. I take it yours wasn't that successful, either." David lounged on the floor, his back propped up by the large leather wing-back chair.

Clay gulped down a few swallows of the cold brew. "We're just friends."

"You're just kidding yourself. I've seen that look before—in the mirror. You're smitten, Clay, and it's bad."

"It'll pass."

"Yup. In about thirty years or so. Give or take a decade."

"Look who's talking," Clay sneered, his frustration topping the scale. "You've been after Laura for years, and once you get close to her, you back off!"

"I know." David sighed, not offended at his friend's accusation. "I'm afraid to press her for more than friendship in case she decides to turn me down and never lets me darken her door again. I'd rather have a small part of Laura forever than force the issue and lose that connection." He stared at his downcast friend. "And you, my friend, are doing the same damn thing. You're just disguising it under other emotions and an engagement you never should have made."

Clay's anger left as quick as it came. "Probably," he finally admitted, feeling better just talking about it. "But I broke up with Magda two weeks ago."

He had David's full attention. "Why? How?"

"I just told her the truth. She and I didn't have what it took to go the distance, and I wasn't ready to commit myself to marriage."

"With her."

He shrugged. "Maybe. I just don't know."

"Katherine gives you a pain in the neck and a bigger one somewhere in the vicinity of the heart?"

"Dammit, yes." His voice was a reluctant growl.

David grinned, but there was sadness in his eyes. "Welcome to my world, friend."

"This is hell."

"You're right," David muttered into his beer can. "And I think it's time I did something about it. Watching you has made me realize just what a coward I've been."

"Glad to help out," Clay retorted dryly.

David chuckled. "A friend in need . . ."

"Now if we could only solve my problems as easily."

"Oh, no. You're going to have to fight your way out of your own confusion. You wouldn't listen to me if I gave you the answer on a platter."

"Try me." Clay's voice held a challenge.

"Marry her."

"Marry in haste, repent in leisure."

"Great. Quote clichés all night long, but don't do what I do, do what I say. Marry her."

"As soon as I see miracles happening on your side of the street."

"You're a fool," David muttered.

"I'm in good company."

"I'll drink to that."

Even with a good friend for company, it was a very lonely night.

WHEN SUNSHINE BLAZED through the patio window, warming Clay's skin, it took him several moments to realize he'd slept on the living room floor. With two aspirin and plenty of orange juice in his system, he made the decision to stay home and do his paperwork in the den. It would keep him out of Katherine's way and in his own cocoon to work out his problems.

But he was just as troubled at eight o'clock that night as he had been at eight o'clock that morning.

KATHERINE'S EMOTIONS plummeted when she realized just how much she had wanted her day to end on a different note. Clay was *supposed* to be at work so she could demonstrate her professional ability! He was *supposed* to admire her from afar and wish she were his full-time secretary. His full-time lover. He was *supposed* to wish for her, and then turn wishes into actions. . . .

So much for suppositions.

After a nerve-racking, very lonely day she stepped inside Laura's house and closed the door, leaning against it.

"Katherine?" Laura called from the living room. "Come join us for a glass of wine."

With a sigh she pushed away from the door and walked slowly into the living room. She smiled briefly at David and accepted the fluted, crystal glass Laura handed her. "Hello, you two."

"You look like hell," Laura said, taking in the tiredness Katherine couldn't hide. "What happened?"

"Clay and I flew to Dallas yesterday and closed a real-estate deal he wanted," she said wearily. "And today he didn't even show up so I could show him how much I wasn't impressed by his business acumen."

David chuckled, absently playing with Laura's hair. Apparently all was well with those two. "Normally he won't take anyone with him in that treasured plane of his. It should make you happy, not sad. And Clay seldom takes anyone on business trips. In fact, I'd say you're the first."

Her green eyes widened for a moment, then her shoulders slumped again. "It was great until we landed back here. Then he withdrew, acting as if I had the mumps or something. He didn't even come to work today."

This time David laughed out loud, a deep belly laugh that reverberated off the walls. "He must really be in deep and fighting it all the way."

"Why?" Both Laura and Katherine stared at him as if he'd grown two heads.

"Why?" David looked at both of them as if they couldn't put two and two together. "Because," he said patiently, "yesterday he wanted Katherine with him badly enough to relax his own rules about mixing business with pleasure, and then he obviously got scared."

Katherine groaned and settled into the chair across from them, curling her toes in the plush carpet. "He's feeling guilty, that's all. If he invited anyone, it should have been Magda."

"Why?" David asked, his expression one of surprise. "Magda's been out of the picture for the past two weeks. He certainly wasn't worried about her."

Katherine leaned forward. "What did you say?"

Laura's hazel eyes pinned him to the couch. "What?"

David had the grace to flush. "Damn! I wasn't supposed to say anything. I forgot."

"Well it's too late to remember that now, so spill the rest of the beans," Laura said grimly. "What happened?"

Running a hand through his mink-dark hair, David sighed heavily. "I knew I should have left while I had the chance."

"If you think you can leave all in one piece after dropping that little bombshell, you're sadly mistaken," Katherine stated between clenched teeth. She already had a good idea what had happened, but wanted it confirmed before she allowed her temper free rein.

David realized when he was beaten. "Clay broke his engagement to Magda about two weeks ago."

"Snake," Katherine muttered.

"Trouble," David said grimly.

"You bet," Katherine answered.

"That turkey," Laura exclaimed.

"I'm sorry," David murmured.

"For whom?" Katherine asked.

"For Clay, knowing you two." David unwound his fingers from Laura's hair and stood. "I think I'd better get going before I get in even more trouble."

"David," Katherine said slowly, her mind racing with possibilities. "If you don't tell Clay you spilled the beans, neither will we." She smiled most beguilingly, but the glint of battle in her eyes was enough to warn even the biggest of fools.

David stared at her for a moment, then shook his head. "Amazing."

"Nothing's amazing. He just needs to think this through and see the light. My light." Her voice was filled with conviction.

"I still say he's scared to death of you and I have a hunch you've got your own plans to take advantage of that."

"Clay needs me, David. He just doesn't know it yet," Katherine explained. David's news was the best she'd heard all week, but that didn't mean she wasn't mad at Clay for not telling her himself. The coward!

"I'm sure you'll be the first to tell him," he commented dryly, holding out his hand and pulling Laura up. "Now walk me to the door and hope that I live through this mess. I can see both your minds working overtime already. It's difficult enough to let the other half of the human race win, I don't have to watch the triumph, too."

Laura chuckled. "Poor defenseless guys. None of you stand a chance against the big bad women."

"You said it," Katherine heard him mutter as Laura walked him outside to his car.

She leaned back in the chair and stared up at the ceiling, attempting to leash her Irish temper enough to come up with a sweet form of revenge.

Automatically, her fingers went to her earlobes to caress the jewels that had been there so long. She met flesh instead of stone and dropped her hand. For just a moment she'd forgotten she'd given them to Clay.

All he saw when he looked at them was their monetary worth, but she felt the loss of the gift itself. Perhaps with time—just perhaps—he would grow to realize that anything given in love is worth ten times more because of its emotional value. After all, her most precious possessions were now in his care: her love and her jewels.

Then she smiled. If Irish elves could really conjure up magic, she was hoping her brand of that commodity would work. Now was the time to move into Magda's empty place in Clay's life. One step at a time.

THE NEXT DAY turned out to be the longest day of Clay's life. Every two minutes he was popping his head into the main office. And every time he did so, Katherine was talking to a different client with one of the salesmen standing by her side, nodding his head as though she were reciting everything exactly the way he would have.

Occasionally he would signal her to come to his office, but her sweet smile aimed his way was the only answer. She never took a step toward him.

He felt frustrated by the end of the morning. Was she purposely ignoring him or was she that busy? Then he'd remind himself that he was the boss and could *order* her to come to his office. Then he remembered he was the boss and needed her to earn her wages. It was good logic, but his mind wasn't listening to logic anymore.

As lunchtime came and went and the morning turned to afternoon, frustration turned to anger. His mind kept retreating to the morning he had picked her up when she was dressed in nothing but a sexy teddy and black hose. And every time he saw her with one of the salesmen, he reconstructed the treasures that were hidden under her demure dress, and the blood in his veins would heat and flow like an out-of-control river.

Even dressed as she was, she was too damned attractive to stay in a roomful of men and not cause a stir. And he didn't like the reactions she was causing, if the look in the men's eyes was any indication.

Consuela occasionally gave him a smug I-told-you-so look, but he ignored her, harboring his own anger as if it were gold. He *liked* feeling angry at Katherine—it freed his emotions even if they were the wrong ones.

Leave it to Consuela to rub salt in his wounds. She slipped into his office and closed the door as if she were conspiring, a cup of fresh coffee and a cookie on a napkin as her excuse. He eyed the cookie warily. "All right. What's the name of this one?"

She smiled smugly. "Patience. It has caramel and pecans in it."

"I should have known." He sighed, biting into it and wishing he had more of its namesake.

When he said no more, she waited, but not for long. She finally said the words she had been communicating with looks all day. "I told you so."

Clay leaned back, tossing his pencil on the desk. "Okay, Consuela. Get it over with."

"Katherine is a natural in sales. She just helped land a contract with that framing corporation to turn that old office building downtown into their headquarters. That's almost a half-a-million-dollar sale."

Half of him was thrilled with the sale, but the other half was as frustrated and angry as before. "With whose help? Are you discounting our own, highly trained sales staff?"

She shrugged. "If the customer had thought the salesman was so good he would have bought the darn building the last two times he's been here, or the first three times he saw the building. But he didn't. He bought today, after Katherine talked to him."

There was nothing more smug than Consuela when she knew she had a strong point. Why he put up with her. . . "He was already presold."

"Huh!" she grunted, her arms crossed to do verbal battle. "Like Oscar Meyer says: 'Bologna.'"

He sighed and pulled himself back up to a straight position. "I'll congratulate her later." Much later, when he could strangle her slender, sexy throat as he politely thanked her for the sale.

"Good. Fair is fair." Consuela uncrossed her arms and reached for the doorknob, silently informing him that she had reached her objective. Now if he could only reach his. Forget that. If he only knew what his objectives were, he'd be miles ahead of both women!

As the door closed behind Consuela, Clay picked up the pencil he had been using and broke it in half, throwing both pieces across the room.

Damn her hide! Every time he turned around, Katherine O'Malley was taunting him, teasing him, making him feel ten feet tall but twice as dumb. And he didn't understand how one woman could do it!

She didn't weave spells or chant incantations, but she was under his skin like a tick and was twice as much of a pest. If he'd learned anything at all from this mess, he'd learned never to pick up a woman at a party. Ever.

The truth was that Clay knew he'd made a mistake in sending Katherine to Laura's house. He just wasn't sure how to get her to come back to his home—and bed—without groveling.

When the knock came, he growled. "Come in!"

Katherine stood in the doorway, her eyes lit with a thousand fires of triumph, her smile a wreath of unbridled happiness that wrapped around his heart. "Did Consuela tell you the good news?" she asked breathlessly, completely ignoring the scowl on his face.

"What good news?"

"I helped Beau sell a half-a-million-dollar building this afternoon!"

"I heard."

"Isn't it wonderful?" She came toward him, stopping only when she reached the side of his desk. "I think I found my calling. Selling is even more fun than being a secretary, not that I know much about either, yet. But I will!"

He leaned back, his hands clutching the wooden arms of his chair. "And what did you promise to do to help get those sales?"

She perched on the side of the desk like a leprechaun. Obviously she didn't realize that the skirt tugged at her hips and showed more of her legs than he had a right to see. And her hands behind her, pressed on the desk meant that the flimsy silk fabric of her dress was pulled taut against her perfectly formed breasts.... He swallowed hard and prayed his libido would die a quick death.

She frowned. "What do you mean?"

"Are you having drinks with the proud owners? Dinner?"

If she hadn't been so excited, she might have noticed the anger he just barely managed to contain. "No," she chuckled, "although he asked. But I have to study every minute of my spare time for night-school classes."

His eyes narrowed. "Just make sure you know what you're selling, Katherine. Some of these men think a pretty smile is an open invitation."

His hints finally sank in. Her movements stilled, her expression glazed with wariness. "What do you mean?"

He leaned forward, his angry face level with her breasts. "Just what I said. They might take your bright smile for another kind of invitation. You have to watch how you come across. Unless of course, you are inviting . . . ?"

Her face whitened, making the tiny freckles that sprinkled her nose stand out. "You think I'm a hooker in disguise? That I'm selling the world's oldest profession, when most men today can get it for free?"

His jealousy wouldn't let him back down. His anger was too deep for that to happen. "Are you?"

Her green eyes gazed back at him, her look as strong and level as his own. "Think hard, Clay, and be careful what you say. What you answer now will determine how our relationship—friendship—whatever you want to call it, will continue. Do you honestly believe that because I would allow *you* into my bed that I want just anybody there? Do you think I'm only looking for a warm body to snuggle up to? That I make declarations of love to every man I meet?"

His eyes roved the length of her body, right down to the tips of her toes. "I don't know. You've never said."

When he looked into her eyes he saw the hurt he had inflicted. A part of him ached to hold her and retract those ugly accusations. But another part wanted to ravish the softness of her body and never let her go. He needed her: to touch, to ignite, to draw the fever from his body and the jealousy that speared his heart. His needs and his anger warred through him.

She took a deep breath, raised her chin and challenged him with green sparks in her eyes. "What would you say if I agreed? That any man would do?"

He was out of his chair in a second. His hands reached under her arms as he lifted her from the top of his desk and pinned her against the wall. Katherine's feet were off the floor, Clay's body pressing intimately against her. His hands strained against her body as he sought the soft places to torment. His warm breath was sharp in her already-ringing ears. "You think you can flirt and tempt with your seductive little movements and not pay up? Is that it?"

Her fingers trembled as she threaded them through his sun-streaked hair. "Are you going make me pay, Clay? For both of us?" she whispered, her mouth unconsciously pouting the words.

He couldn't help it. His need overpowered his anger and he let go of what little control he had. Groaning, he pressed his mouth against hers, his tongue plundering the tender inside of her mouth. Their breath caught and mingled, creating more heat than he could stand. His body was on fire. He shook with the need to touch her flesh, to feel the softness of her beneath his hands. Beneath his body. His heartbeat raced even more with that thought.

"You're a witch," he muttered roughly, his lips still touching hers, brushing tantalizingly back and forth.

"I love you so much," she murmured softly. "Let me be with you, Clay. I won't gripe or complain. I understand now."

Her voice was a whisper, but her words shouted in his ears. "What do you mean?" His voice was like a soft rasp as his lips sought the pulse at her throat. But sirens were going off in his head. Warning. Warning.

"I love you and I'm willing to settle for a small part of your life." Her wide eyes were the color of forest fern as she stared up at him. "Any part you're willing to share with me."

Emotional blackmail, dressed in pretty words. "You'd settle for being the other woman?"

She nodded her head, her eyes wide.

"What is it that you think I need, Katherine?" His hands tightened on her ribs, his fingers working magic.

"Someone who cares enough to make you content." Her answer was simplicity itself. Damn her. She was absolutely right. And the one thing that would make him feel content also happened to be the same thing he was so afraid of: commitment. Mental, physical, metaphysical commitment.

Katherine needed all that, while he couldn't handle those emotions at all. It didn't make it any easier to know that he couldn't let her go, either. Not yet.

Anger rose like bile in his throat. "So one hand washes the other, right? In exchange for certain favors from you, I'm supposed to be responsible for your welfare. Is that what you want?"

Again she nodded, but he could see the lack of conviction in her eyes. He took a deep breath and let her down slowly so her toes could finally touch the floor. Taking a step back, he surveyed her. "It means that you're mine for as long as I say. You can't see anyone else. Not as long as we're together."

Her chin rose at that defiant angle he was beginning to know so well. "Of course." Her teeth were clamped together. "And vice versa."

"Very well," he said distantly, holding her in her place instead of pulling her into his arms again. His eyes focused over her shoulder. He couldn't afford to look at her, to see the hurt in her eyes. "It's four o'clock. I'll be at your place at ten. Meanwhile, get your hair fixed and buy some more sophisticated clothes. I like a sexy woman who is well-groomed. Take my car and get going."

Katherine shook her head as if awakening from a bad dream. Her anger finally bubbled over. She snapped her fingers. "Just like that? Get your hair done and buy sexy clothing, then wait for me to show up?"

"Just like that." His voice was harsh, definite. "Are you still interested?"

Barely banked fury blazed out of eyes that had been soft with passion just moments ago. "Oh, yes, Mr. Reynolds. I'm interested."

"Good." He dropped the Porsche's keys into her palm, careful not to touch her. "Take these."

The heat of her anger continued to seethe through her limbs. She clutched the keys until they bit into her flesh. Without another word, she turned. She needed to get out of there before she took his beautiful antique vase from the side cabinet and slammed him over the head with it!

"Wait." He reached into his desk drawer and pulled out several charge cards, placing them in her hand, also. "Take these, too."

Katherine strode serenely out of the office, but the door crashed back into its frame.

IT'S A WILD, WILD, WONDERFUL
FREE OFFER!

HERE'S WHAT YOU GET:

1. *Four New Harlequin Temptation® Novels—FREE!* Everything comes up hearts and diamonds with four exciting romances — yours FREE from Harlequin Reader Service. Each of these brand-new novels brings you the passion and tenderness of today's greatest love stories.

2. *A Useful, Practical Digital Clock/Calendar—FREE!* As a free gift simply to thank you for accepting four free books we'll send you a stylish digital quartz clock/calendar — a handsome addition to any decor! The changeable, month-at-a-glance calendar pops out, and may be replaced with a favorite photograph.

3. *An Exciting Mystery Bonus—FREE!* You'll go wild over this surprise gift. It will win you compliments and score as a splendid addition to your home.

4. *Money-Saving Home Delivery!* Join Harlequin Reader Service and enjoy the convenience of previewing four new books every month, delivered to your home. Each book is yours for $2.24—26 cents less per book than what you pay in stores. And there is no extra charge for postage and handling. Great savings and total convenience are the name of the game at Harlequin!

5. *Free Newsletter!* It makes you feel like a partner to the world's most popular authors...tells about their upcoming books...even gives you their recipes!

6. *More Mystery Gifts Throughout the Year!* No joke! Because home subscribers are our most valued readers, we'll be sending you additional free gifts from time to time—as a token of our appreciation!

GO WILD
WITH HARLEQUIN TODAY—
JUST COMPLETE, DETACH AND
MAIL YOUR FREE-OFFER CARD!

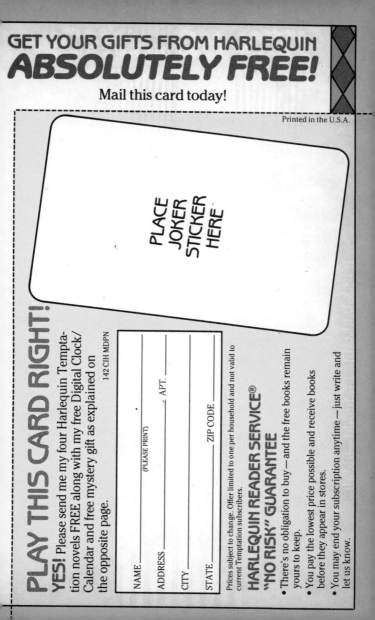

GET YOUR GIFTS FROM HARLEQUIN
ABSOLUTELY FREE!

Mail this card today!

Printed in the U.S.A.

PLACE
JOKER
STICKER
HERE

PLAY THIS CARD RIGHT!

YES! Please send me my four Harlequin Temptation novels FREE along with my free Digital Clock/ Calendar and free mystery gift as explained on the opposite page.

142 CIH MDPN

NAME _____
(PLEASE PRINT)

ADDRESS _____ APT. _____

CITY _____

STATE _____ ZIP CODE _____

Prices subject to change. Offer limited to one per household and not valid to current Temptation subscribers.

HARLEQUIN READER SERVICE® "NO RISK" GUARANTEE

- There's no obligation to buy — and the free books remain yours to keep.
- You pay the lowest price possible and receive books before they appear in stores.
- You may end your subscription anytime — just write and let us know.

IT'S NO JOKE!

MAIL THE POSTPAID CARD AND
GET FREE GIFTS AND $10.00 WORTH OF
HARLEQUIN NOVELS — *FREE!*

8

KATHERINE AIMED the gleaming black Porsche toward North Star Mall, her anger apparent in every line of her body.

So he wanted to *pay* for her love, did he? Well, that's what he'd do—that egotistical monster!

Sure, she had offered herself to him. More than once. But she hadn't expected him to take her up on it! He was supposed to confess that Magda wasn't for him, and that Katherine fit him to a tee! He was supposed to apologize to her for wasting all this time, then take her in his arms and confess his love for her. He was supposed to have told her the truth about his aborted engagement!

What had gone wrong?

It didn't matter. The plan had backfired, and now she had to figure out how to open his eyes and see her as the only woman for him. Her eyes narrowed. Clay thought he wanted a kept woman—she'd show him a kept woman.

She remembered something Laura had once quoted and laughed. "Be careful what you wish for—you just might get it."

Laura. As soon as she was in the mall, she'd call her. Laura would know what needed to be done besides spend every dime she could on clothing. There had to be something Katherine could do to make Clay realize just how stupid he was acting! And Laura knew him best.

"Mr. Reynolds," she whispered into the interior as she pulled in front of the Frost Brothers store. "You're gonna get more than you bargained for. I'm worth a lot more than you know. I guar-an-tee."

CLAY RENTED a two-door Lincoln whose seat could be adjusted to sit as high as Katherine needed it to be and drove home. It would be waiting for her when he took her back to his home tonight.

Opening his front door, he stepped in and felt the blast of chilled air on his face and neck. He needed to relax and sort through some thoughts and problems that were clamoring for release.

After the heat of the outside, the house was almost too cool. It was also empty and quiet as death. He felt as if he were walking into a tomb, which underlined just how lonely he was. Until Katherine came into his life, he had thought he loved and needed this peace, but now it felt as though some vital life-force was gone. He had taunted both of them because of his own basic insecurities, now it was time to come clean and face a few home truths . . . right after he figured out what those truths were.

At least he'd gotten his wish without groveling. Katherine would be back in his home—and his bed— tonight. But he wasn't too proud of how he'd managed it. Desperation was a strange slave driver.

But before he fixed himself a drink, got a bite to eat or sat down on the couch, he reached for the jeweled earrings kept tucked in the small wall safe in his den. With them clasped securely in his hand, he sat in the wing-back chair and stared at the woodland scene outside his window.

KATHERINE DROPPED DOWN on the couch and leaned her head back. Eyes closed, she allowed the coolness of Laura's house to surround her, finally breathing without feeling as if she were in an oven. The early June heat had been unbearable as she paced the parking lot trying to remember where she had parked the sleek Porsche. She had had too much on her mind to remember the exact location, and anger and frustration with Clay had erased any memory she might have had.

She opened one eye and glanced down at her purchases. At least fifteen boxes and bags were piled high on the carpet. They held three designer gowns, five expensive but casual outfits, a few day dresses, several teddies and nightgowns in various shades of jewel tones and high heels that cost more than a hundred dollars apiece.

She had done exactly what he had requested and spent money on his credit cards. Thousands of dollars. The only thing that kept guilt from baying at her mind's door was that he had her jewels, which she now knew were worth triple what she could ever owe him. But from now on, she vowed, she'd never let her temper get the best of her. She couldn't afford all this debt.

Still in the throes of anger, she'd gone the rest of the nine yards and got a manicure, pedicure, facial and new hairstyle. Carlo, the hairdresser, had bright brown eyes that had lit up with the challenge before him. He had practically rubbed his hands together in glee.

"You must tame your hair to do what you want, but you must never take away its spirit!" he exclaimed with a slight lisp as he trimmed and cut and shaped. And he had been right. The hairdo was a masterpiece and well worth the exorbitant amount he had charged. Wild, casually curled, it was beautiful, but Katherine wasn't sure she could duplicate what Carlo had created.

At least it would last for tonight.

Both eyes opened with that thought. She had to get ready!

She gathered the packages in her arms and rushed to her bedroom, only to drop them on the floor as she reached for the oversize brown manila envelope perched on her pillow. Laura had scrawled Katherine's name across the front of it, and she frowned as she opened the flap, wondering what on earth Laura had done now.

Her frown turned to a grin and the grin to laughter. The note inside gave the explanation.

Katherine—Clay has always had others sign one of these, so turnabout's fair play. Use in case of emergency. Maybe it will be the very thing to wake him up. Good luck!

CLAY STEPPED OUT of the cab and stared at Laura's front door. A quick glance at his Porsche sitting in the driveway told him she had managed the powerful car without denting it. The Lincoln he had rented that afternoon was waiting at home for her. The key was under her pillow.

A shadowy form passed by the window, and Clay recognized it as Katherine's. Something about her drove him to the edge of frustration and back. She kept him in a constant state of turmoil, forcing him out of control in any situation where she was involved. Now, after several hours of soul-searching he knew himself better. He finally admitted—at least to himself—that he loved her.

He couldn't believe what he had done today, goading her and then throwing the cards and keys at her. She had declared her love for him so openly, so honestly, without all the machinations that other women he'd know had gone through. But then, she had always been that way. On any topic. There wasn't a lying bone in her body. She wanted him—and he was trying to punish her because he wanted her, too. But because their needs would put conditions on both of them, he couldn't let this relationship get out of hand. Conditions. Restrictions. The two words he hated most.

He walked up the sidewalk, his eyes seeking her through the filmy curtains. By the time he knocked, he was impatient to see her, be with her, talk to her and, perhaps, just once, get her under control so he could feel secure again.

But when she opened the door, he knew it wasn't to be.

She was wearing a filmy, midnight-blue blouse that hugged her slim shoulders and small breasts. Matching slacks outlined the rest of her beguiling figure. Her makeup was flawless, her lips full and pouting and damp, as if she had just darted her small tongue across them. Her hair billowed softly about her shoulders, and he itched to run his fingers through it. But it was her smile that stopped him in his tracks. "I thought you'd never get here," she said breathlessly.

"I'm early." His voice was barely above a whisper.

"I know, but it doesn't feel like it."

She opened the door wider and he stepped inside, closing it behind him and wondering how he was going to gain control of the situation. Not one idea came to mind, but those thoughts that did spring into his head filled his body with a tension that was almost unbearable.

They walked into the living room, Clay clenching his hands to rid himself of the urge to grab and hold her close. He wanted to absorb her so he'd never be without her again.

He could feel his body tighten, readying.... He turned and faced her. "Are you still willing to go through with this new relationship?" His voice was rough, demanding.

She nodded and her hair caught the glint of the lamp glow.

"Even though I'm marrying someone else and may never change my plans?" he goaded.

Her eyes narrowed slightly, her chin lifted an inch or so, but she nodded again.

"And what do you get out of this?"

She walked toward him until they were toe-to-toe, her eyes softening to a luminous shade of sea-fern. "You," she said softly, placing her small hand on his pounding heart.

He swallowed, then swallowed again. His heartbeat accelerated with her touch, and he knew she could feel it in the center of her palm.

Her green eyes widened and he was almost lost in them. "Is that because of me?"

"Yes." His voice was gruff.

"Do you react to every woman this way?"

His hands stayed clenched at his sides. "No."

"Why me, then?" Her other hand touched his chest, lightly pressing against his nipple.

"You know why." His voice was short, slipped.

"Are you angry?"

"Yes."

"With me?"

A grimace crossed his face. "With both of us."

"Why?" She frowned in confusion. Her tongue darted out to skim her upper lip.

He couldn't resist any longer. His hands spanned her waist, his fingers caressing the skin beneath the flimsy material. She was so small, so soft. So sensuous.

Her eyelids drifted down, a small smile barely tilting the corners of her full, parted mouth. "Clay?" she whispered, and he accepted the question with an answer of his own.

"You tempt too much," he growled accusingly as his lips covered hers, a moan echoing from his throat at the triumph of claiming her mouth as his prize.

It was heaven and hell together as he pressed her closer, devouring her will with his mouth. Then she answered his unrestrained passion with her own, her arms circling his neck as if to pull him closer to her.

Their tongues dueled and they savored the overwhelming passion they had unleashed. Their kisses were speaking a language they each understood completely.

Reaching down, he cupped her buttocks in the palms of his hands, raising and pressing her against him, showing her his almost overwhelming need. When he lifted his mouth from hers, his breath was hot, searing her with unspent passion. "Every time I'm near you, I go a little insane," he muttered hoarsely. "I react to you as I've never reacted to a woman before—and I hate it." His damp forehead was pressed against hers as he tried to catch his breath and straighten out his jumbled thoughts. "It's just not fair, Katherine."

Her husky chuckle filled his mind. "I could say the same thing, Clay, but I won't. You already have a big head."

His brows rose. "I might be sure of myself in business, but never when I'm around you. You send me spinning off balance."

Her fingers traced the strong line of his jaw then his soft lips, her eyes drinking in everything she touched. "I love you."

He stilled, finally willing to accept her declaration. "How do you know?"

She clasped his hand to her breast, and he could feel her quickened heartbeat. "I just do."

His frown stopped her fingers from traveling further, and when he spoke his voice was laced with sadness. "I've never believed in love, Katherine. It always seemed more like an emotional trap than something wonderful."

"You don't chalk all this emotion up to chemistry, do you?" She tried to sound as if she was kidding, but her voice broke on the last two words, telling him just how important his answer was to her.

He tried to form the right words, but nothing came. He'd never been able to say the words before, and they wouldn't come forth now. The silence stretched.

"Clay?"

He shook his head, more from confusion than to form a negative answer. "I don't know, honey. I just don't know anymore."

Her hand covered his own heart, her small palm seeming even smaller against the breadth of his chest. "So you've never been in love?" He knew she could feel his response to her touch.

"No."

"What about Magda?"

He sighed, pulling away from her, only to feel the coldness of her absence in his arms. He'd deceived her long enough, but this wasn't the time to discuss it. Later. After he made love to her, he'd explain it all. Perhaps then he'd at least have more control over her temper. A small voice inside him laughed hysterically. There was no controlling her, let alone her temper. "Change the subject."

She touched his arm. "I'm sorry, Clay, but she isn't right."

"And you are?" he chided gently.

She nodded, her hair brushing gently against her collarbones. "I think so. But if I'm not, it still doesn't mean she's right for you. It's not a question of one or the other. This isn't multiple choice, where there's a right answer or a grade score."

He couldn't help the rueful smile that claimed his mouth. "You certainly get to the point."

"So do you, when it concerns business." *But not our love,* her eyes seemed to say. "Clay," she began as he brushed away a tendril of her hair, then allowed his fingers to play with the silken strand.

He smiled sadly. "I've never seen anything but hurt in the name of love. I'll never say the words, Katherine. If you can't handle that, let's call it quits now, before you get hurt."

"Would you mind if I was hurt?" she asked softly.

"Yes." His voice was gruff.

"Why?"

"Because I have enough on my conscience already. I don't want to add you, too." He cupped her face with his hands. "I want you so badly I ache, but I can't guarantee I'll feel the same way after I've held you in my arms night after night. I might want to walk away."

She flinched, but knew he was right. At least he was honest. "And you couldn't do that with a clear conscience if I was hurt?"

"No."

She gave a heavy sigh before staring up at him again, her love shining enough to warm him all over. "I won't make it easy for you, Clay. I love you and I want to be with you. I want to touch you, hold you against my breast while you sleep. I want you to need me just as much as I need you, but I won't hang on if—or when—you say it's over. I have my pride, too."

He pulled her back into his arms. "Oh, Katherine," he groaned. "What the hell am I going to do with you?"

"Take me home and love me until dawn?" she whispered, wrapping her arms around his waist and tilting her face toward him as if he were the sun and she a flower. Possessiveness flowed through him, filling him with the need to keep her safe. Keep her in his arms. Keep her...

He shook his head again, only this time it was to shake out the nebulous ideas that were forming in the back of his mind. "Pack a bag, Katherine. We're leaving."

A smile slowly lit up her face and it warmed him all the way to his toes.

"Yes, sir," she murmured, placing a quick kiss on the corner of his mouth, tempting him almost beyond reason. Then she slipped out of his arms before he could grab her again, disappearing down the hallway toward her room.

It took every ounce of restraint he had to stand rooted to the spot instead of following and wrestling her to the floor, taking instant gratification. He could wait. He would wait. He was a man, not an animal.

He hoped he knew the difference, but he wasn't sure anymore.

KATHERINE'S INSIDES WERE SHAKING, but she ignored it. She had asked for Clay's love. She had begged to be a part of his life, and there was no reason to back out now, not when she was so close to what her heart desired. She was taking a gamble—one that she might lose—but there was no other choice left to her. For Katherine, it was either Clay or no one at all.

She glanced at him. The dimness of the car hid the grim creases around his mouth that had been there ever since she had walked back into the room, Laura's overnight suitcase in her hand.

He'd barely spoken since. She continued to watch him even though she made note of the direction they were headed. They had just turned off Loop 610 and curved toward Dominion Country Club. Soon they'd be at his town house.

She shivered.

"Cold?" He reached for the heater switch, but her hand covered his instead. He turned his palm over and captured her.

"No, I'm fine." She held on tight, afraid to let go just yet. His thumb began gently rubbing against her fingers, sending shivers up and down her spine.

"How do you feel?" he asked, really wondering whether or not she wanted to back out of this insane near relationship.

"Like a hot-fudge sundae."

His brows rose in question, his brown eyes darting to hers.

"I'm both hot and cold at the same time, waiting for the first bite to be taken." Her smile was stiff, and he squeezed her hand.

"I promise I won't jump your bones the minute we walk through the door."

"I wish you would."

"Why?"

She chuckled nervously. "Because then this tension would be over and I'd relax and enjoy your company."

He frowned. "If you don't want to follow through with this, just say so." His voice was clipped.

"I do," she whispered, her hand tightening on his. "I'm just nervous."

"We've done this before, Katherine," he reminded her.

"I remember," she chuckled ruefully. "But we didn't know we'd wind up that way. This time it's . . . it's . . ."

"Calculated?"

"Planned," she corrected softly.

He pulled off the highway and onto the access road, his hand leaving hers to grip the steering wheel. She waited—and prayed—that he would take her hand again, but he didn't. Her heart beat hard against her ribs. She was doing this all wrong. She should be seducing him, heaping praises upon his golden head, throwing grapes into his mouth and fanning his body with palm fronds.

A grin teased the corners of her mouth at the thought of him playing Julius Caesar to her Cleopatra. He'd make an autocratic Julius and she certainly was no Cleopatra!

"The first planned time is the most awkward, you know," she said aloud, reassuring herself far more than him.

"Is that right?"

"Oh, yes," she went on breezily. "After that, everything's a snap." She clicked her fingers as if to prove the point.

He chuckled. "You're incorrigible."

"No, but you're helping me become that way," she teased.

"I'm not too sure it's not the other way around."

"You? Innocent? Me, the seducer?" She pretended to think a moment. "Why not?"

Traffic became congested as cars backed up for all the lights through subdivision after subdivision and he looked over at her, curiosity lighting his eyes. "How would you seduce me?"

"Well," she said slowly. "First I'd kiss you, finding all the secret places in your mouth that others might not have found. I'd feel your tongue against mine, feel the way you grew against my stomach when we're pressed together as I aroused you.

"I'd kiss your eyelids closed, then trail kisses down your jaw and nibble on your neck, smelling the scent of that after-shave you wear. Your ears would be moist with my whispered words of passion." She hesitated for a moment, then continued in an even lower tone. "I'd feel so close and need you so much that I'd have to rub against you, wanting you to be as close to me as you could get, knowing that you were craving the same thing I was. My hands would run through your hair, around the muscles in your neck and arms. I'd be hoping you were as ready for me as I was for you, but I'd wait until you felt empty and aching before I'd make my next move."

He cleared his throat. "Which is?"

"I'd undo your shirt buttons one by one, kissing every inch of skin as I went. I'd take your shirt off your shoulders, but I'd leave the cuffs buttoned so your arms were forced to hang at your side. You'd be unable to touch, to feel, to lead. . . ."

The car jumped forward and he muttered something under his breath as he began the snail's march to the next light. She heard his shallow breathing and knew she'd hit a nerve—the same one that was making her breathless.

"I'd find each rib and indentation because you'd be my prisoner, mine to do with what I want. My fingers would run through your hair, feeling the texture and weight of it. I'd bury my face in your chest and let the curly strands tickle my nose. And then I'd capture your nipple with my mouth. You'd struggle a little, but your cuffs would hold you secure in my grasp."

A horn honked and Clay cursed under his breath as he stopped for another red light.

She stared at him, blotting out everything but his body, his tension, his tight expression. His teeth were clenched, the small muscle by his jaw ticked like a meter. "Go on," he gritted.

She smiled triumphantly, feeling a power she'd never known before. He didn't want to listen, but he was responding anyway, against his will.

"I'd reach for your belt and unbuckle it, then unsnap your pants, letting them drop to the floor and cuff your legs so you couldn't walk away. My hands would slip underneath the elastic of your briefs while my mouth found your navel."

"Enough!" he practically yelled as he turned onto the street that led to his house. His knuckles were white against the black of the steering wheel. There was a pinched look around his mouth, almost as if he was in some kind of pain.

"Don't you want to hear the rest?" Her voice was as breathless as his.

"Hold that thought," he said through clenched teeth.

Driving up to the house, he reached for the garage door opener on his sun visor and pushed the button with an angry jab. Katherine leaned against her headrest, closing her eyes. She forced herself to drop the images she had created for Clay, making herself calm once more. Sanity returned slowly, bringing her surroundings back into focus. She'd blown it. She'd gone too far. Where had she found the nerve to *say* those things?

They pulled into the garage and the door came down behind them, leaving them in darkness. Clay turned to her, his voice rasping in the sudden quiet. "Katherine," he began.

But she was quicker. She opened the door and stepped out, standing by the side of the car. Her legs felt like rubber, her hands still shaking, only now they were shaking because of the erotic pictures she had painted. Her whole body was hot and spineless, and she clung to the door, praying he wouldn't vent his anger yet. Not until she was seated in the well-lit house and able to compose her features into some expression besides one of deep emotional hunger.

Without another word he stepped from the car and reached for her bag in the back seat. Then he flipped on the light and led her into the kitchen, closing the garage door behind him with a thud and a snap as he locked it securely.

She wanted to run, but she wasn't sure in which direction: toward him or away from him. The way her emotions were jumbled right now she could flip a coin and willingly do either one.

Clay walked toward her determinedly, not stopping until he almost touched her. Her eyes were wide, her lips parted as she stared up at him. He was so big, so strong, so—

His lips covered hers, sending his moan into the back of her throat as he devoured her with an appetite that knew no bounds. His roughness, his open, obvious arousal was an aphrodisiac to her. Her fingers clung to the back of his shirt as she answered him with the same desperate fierceness. Her tongue dueled with his before gentling and letting him take command.

He softened, too, savoring her taste, the strokes of his tongue slowing to imitate the actions of lovemaking. He clasped one breast in his hand, cupping her nipple in his palm and circling her flesh gently, teasing her to a heated pitch she didn't know was possible.

He nibbled her bottom lip. "You're an enchantress."

"You're Merlin."

"You're mine!" he said before claiming her mouth again, this time branding her with possession. She didn't know when her shirt was unbuttoned and removed, but the coolness of the air conditioning was a stark contrast to the heat of his touch. She snuggled closer to his hand, bringing forth soft murmurs that echoed in her throat.

He picked her up and carried her into his room, not letting her go until they reached the bed. Placing her in the center, Clay stood back, his eyes narrowed as he took in her disheveled appearance. "You look like you've already been made passionate love to."

"You don't," she said, finally finding her voice. She leaned back on her elbows and stared at him, not bothered that she was nearly naked from the waist up. "You're too dressed."

Without taking his eyes from her, he unbuttoned his shirt, then slipped it off, wadded it up and threw it in the corner. His buckle clicked, his snap unsnapped, his zipper unzipped. In one motion his pants and briefs were on the floor and he stepped out of them. He slipped off his shoes and yanked at the socks until both were disposed of, then stood magnificently naked as her eyes played over his strong, bare flesh.

"Are you frightened?" His voice was soft, and if she didn't know better, she would have thought he was vulnerable . . . as vulnerable as she was.

"No," she whispered. "Just unsure. Everything's so different."

He smiled and the whole room lit up. "And so wonderful. This time it isn't an accident of hormones,

Katherine. We both know what we're doing, with no excuses except that we want each other," he said. He stretched out next to her, his eyes telling her even more than his words. With infinite gentleness he began the delightfully slow process of uncovering her partially clad body.

Her pants landed on the floor by his pants, her bra hit the side of the wall and disappeared behind the bed. She reached for the lacy edge of her panties, but he stopped her. "Not yet, sweet."

She halted, opening her eyes dreamily. "Won't it make it, uh, difficult this way?"

He chuckled, bending to tease the softness of her breast. "Interesting, to say the least."

His hand trailed over the flat planes of her stomach, then dropped to the feminine mound, and she couldn't hold in the light sigh that escaped. "That's it, darling, let the feeling overpower you," he murmured before finally capturing a rose-colored bud in his mouth and sucking gently in unison with his hand movement. She tasted like soft night flowers. So good. So very good.

Her own hands reached for him, trailing down to his taut stomach. Hearing him catch his breath at her touch made her even more brave. She wrapped her small hand around him, feeling the size and slick texture of his manhood. His moan fed her desire to learn more, but he grasped her hand, bringing it intimately back to her own body. "Show me. Show me what pleases you most."

She bit her lower lip. "I can't," she whispered, hoping he would understand.

"Shh," he reassured her, his lips scant inches from her ear. "It's all right. You will. Later."

Finally he slipped his hand underneath the elastic and found the moist warmth of her. She moved against his palm, her lips parting, her eyes half closed, consumed by the desire he'd awakened in her.

He sought her breast again, tugging at the budding softness with his mouth until he could feel it harden against his tongue. Her whole body tightened in expectation, but he refused to relent.

"Please," she moaned and he knew what she wanted, but wasn't yet ready to end his own torture. Katherine first. His Katherine . . .

She arched her back and a tense smile played over his mouth. His own body was drawn as taut as a bow string stretched to the limit.

As she reached the pinnacle, he encased himself in her, resting his weight on his arms as he took the first sweet plunge into the tight sheath of her body.

If he had ever doubted the existence of heaven, he knew better now. Heaven was in Katherine's arms.

9

CLAY PROWLED the darkness of his house, his naked body blending with the shadows and silence. A glance at the clock told him it was three in the morning, but his brain was as alert as if it were dawn and he was waking from an eight-hour sleep.

Katherine lay asleep in his bed, the sheet barely covering her trim buttocks. He couldn't help but look in every once in a while and make sure that she was still there. Waiting for him.

What a mess. Other women had thrown themselves at him for one reason or another, and he'd always been in control. Never, never would he have proposed such a ludicrous relationship to them.

Mistress. The word left a bad taste in his mouth. Live-in meant that she would share living and loving space with him. But mistress. That implied she was paid to work. In his bed. Exclusively.

Emotions flooded him at that thought. Oh, that's where he wanted her to be, all right. In his bed and no one else's. He wanted her there in the evening and waking with him in the morning. He craved her arms around him at every moment, stroking him, petting him, soothing him. Loving him.

Earlier, when he'd finally pulled the car key out from under the pillow, he didn't know who was more embarrassed. She had mumbled her thanks and he had nodded his welcome.

They made quite a pair. Both were embarrassed with the situation. Katherine because it went against what she thought was love, and Clay because he wasn't sure what love was or how long it lasted. Consequently they both wanted something that was elusive.

He needed her to be there because she *wanted* to be, not because he was wealthy enough to afford her. And yet *he* was the one putting a price tag on his need of her. If she were any other woman it wouldn't bother him. But Katherine was different.

He hadn't cared enough for Magda to be frightened of the future. But it was as if Katherine held a marriage license in one hand and a leash in the other. The leash was for him.

He needed his freedom. *To do what?* a little voice asked.

To breathe, he answered, feeling the tension build inside him again. *To do what I want to do whenever I want to do it.*

But you won't let her have the same options! the voice chided. The voice was right. He'd die if he thought someone else touched her, held her, laughed with her in the dark of night. Loved her.

Love. He hated that word with a passion. Love was a patsy's word. It meant giving up all rights to do what he wanted and putting his emotional fate and happiness in someone else's hands. And that someone else might be kind, but they could be cruel. The end result was the same: he would lose control of his own life.

A sigh swept through the darkness to reach his ears and he strode to the door of his bedroom to check on her. The sheet had worked down to tangle in her legs, giving him a view of her slim waist and a sweetly rounded rump. So beautiful . . .

To hell with trying to analyze his situation in the middle of the night. Tomorrow was plenty of time. Right now he needed to be next to her, to reassure himself that she was really here, in his home and his care.

He slipped his feet under the sheet and reached out, pulling her sleeping form toward his. She turned, curling around the trunk of his body like a kitten wrapped around a ball of yarn. Her hand rested on his chest and he covered it with his own, then sighed and closed his eyes, more peaceful than he'd ever been before.

When the alarm went off, he awoke to find her gone. Her absence left a huge hole in the fabric of his contentment. A note was on her pillow and he squinted to read it.

Call me whenever you need me.

He crumpled the note in his fist, but it didn't make the loneliness any easier to bear.

CONSUELA EYED both Katherine and Clay narrowly as she answered the ringing phones. Very little got by the astute woman, but for once Clay hoped she'd keep her mouth closed. Katherine had been shy and nervous ever since she'd shown up in the office, and he didn't think she needed to have anything else upset her.

After fighting with himself all day, he finally gave in to his own demands as the office was about to close. He called Katherine into his office.

Staring out the window because he didn't trust himself not to reach for her, he spoke. "From now on I want you to spend the full night with me. I don't want you leaving without my knowing."

She took a step toward him, then stopped. He could smell her perfume and it wrapped around his senses. "If that's what you want."

"It is."

After a moment's hesitation, she slid her arms around his waist, her head resting against his back. "I'll see you again in an hour," she said softly, giving a quick, light squeeze.

Then she was gone. Clay rocked on his heels, feeling inordinately proud of himself. That had been almost painless.

She went to his house shortly after work, her suitcase in her hand.

Clay cooked dinner, then helped clean up—talking all the time. It was odd, but he'd never felt so free to express opinions with someone before. Her laughter rang in his head, her smiles lit his own eyes.

That night he undressed her slowly, savoring every movement. When they were both naked, he opened the drawer and drew out the earrings he'd been keeping for her. With hands that were tender, he placed them where they belonged—competing for beauty with her eyes.

They made love tenderly, saying with their hands and bodies what was never even whispered. Then they fell asleep locked in each other's arms until morning and the outside world and work intruded upon their world.

CONSUELA HANDED him a small stack of messages, then pushed the plate of goodies toward him. Clay sniffed. "What are they?"

"They're called temptation tarts. My next door neighbor, Vicky, always makes them."

His eyes darted up, narrowing. Consuela's expression was innocence personified. Katherine turned away, slipping her purse in the drawer without looking at either of them.

"I'll pass." He retreated to his office, just barely resisting the urge to slam the door.

All of Katherine's senses were focused on Clay until his office door was quietly closed behind him. Too quietly. Her shoulders sagged with the weight of his indifference. She knew. She knew he was afraid of love, afraid of commitment. Afraid of her.

A small part of her wanted him to feel that way; it meant that he cared at least a little. Maybe even a lot. But the other part, the bigger part, realized that he might run as far away from her as he could go. And that thought frightened *her*.

She loved him. After last night she realized just how much. Her feelings were just as committed as if words from a preacher had been spoken. A terrible sadness invaded her. She had to face the fact that her love was one-sided. He would never let the barriers down enough to allow her into his life. His heart. Never.

"Katherine?" Consuela's voice filtered through all her thoughts, and she raised her head from the file she had been staring at but not seeing.

"Yes?"

"Beau wants to go over the contracts from that big sale the other day. That way you'll be able to follow what happens after the initial sale."

She smiled woodenly. "Sure. Thanks."

The older woman lifted up the box of cookies and offered her one. "And have one of these. You never know."

Katherine shrugged, but she knew there was hopelessness in her eyes. "Why not? I've got nothing to lose."

"No, not much, eh?" Consuela muttered, watching the young girl turn and walk toward the sales room. Her head went from side to side as she said a quick prayer in Spanish. But the prayer wasn't for the young girl. It was for a boss who wore blinders and still stubbornly thought he could view the entire world with that handicap.

CLAY SENT OUT for lunch, keeping his door closed to the outside world unless it intruded through the telephone. The less he saw of Katherine right now the better off he was. He needed time to think, to absorb the massive changes he'd gone through since he'd met and gotten involved with her.

He felt as if he'd turned a corner in his life and suddenly he couldn't recognize the streets or the neighborhood. He was lost.

At least two hundred times that day he rose from his chair intending to stride into the outer office and sweep the Irish imp into the circle of his arms and find peace there. Another hundred times he thought of calling her on the intercom and demanding she join him in the privacy of his office. By the end of the day he was exhausted from the effort of denying himself that which he wanted the most: Katherine Maureen O'Malley.

And he wasn't even sure why he was putting himself through the torture.

When his watch read five o'clock, he knew his waiting was over. He strode out the door, flicking his gaze toward her like a whip. "Ready?" he barked, frustration making his voice harsh.

She nodded, placing the last file in the cabinet and shutting the door.

"Don't forget your classes, Katherine. They're very important to a career. You never know when you'll need all that schooling to fall back on," Consuela stated, her back ramrod straight as she shot a disapproving look toward her boss.

He ignored her. "Do you have night school?"

Katherine nodded, her red hair caressing her shoulders and neck, just the way his hands itched to.

"I'll drop you off."

Again she nodded, and he held the door open for her. Watching her walk out, he felt himself hardening right under his secretary's eyes and there wasn't a damn thing he could do about it. Katherine's walk was sheer seduction of the senses.

"Good night, boss," Consuela sang.

His answer was a look that said he knew she knew and he didn't care.

"Where is your class?" He started the car and let the hot air blow out the windows at the same time the cold air came blowing out of the vents. Another sweltering San Antonio day.

"San Antonio College." She spoke quietly. Her hands on her lap were primly held together. "Tonight is beginning algebra."

"Fine." He put the car in gear and revved the engine; it still didn't match the power of his own inner motor. "When you're through we'll grab a bite to eat."

"I can make something when we get back to the town house, Clay. After all, I was a short-order cook and waitress far longer than I was a kid."

He stared straight ahead. "All right."

When they reached the entrance, Clay pulled over, but didn't park. He halted her movement to leave. "I'll be back at this same spot in ninety minutes." It sounded more like a warning than a statement.

She smiled, but the sadness that had been in her eyes all day was still there tonight. "Give me five minutes or so to get out of class."

"Right here," he said again, ignoring her plea for extra minutes.

Her hand came up and cradled his jaw, her fingers playing along his skin. He turned his head and kissed her palm, his tongue stroking the center. Her breath escaped and excitement seared through him, fed by the knowledge of the potency they created between them. Sexual power to be sure, but at least she wasn't the only one with the ability to upset and confuse.

"See you then," she whispered, and her hand dropped to the door latch. Then she was gone, striding up the wide sidewalk toward the opened doors. She was fascinating to watch....

He was double-parked and a horn honking reminded him of it. With short, stabbing movements he turned the car into the lane of traffic and drove around the downtown campus to a chain restaurant that specialized in breakfast twenty-four hours a day.

Reading his copy of the *Wall Street Journal* and ordering a cup of coffee helped to relieve those first few minutes of emptiness that he felt every time Katherine left his side. All he had to do was fill the next eighty-five minutes and then he'd have her back where she belonged.

It was the longest eighty-five minutes of his life. Students filled and emptied the booths, laughing and joking with their friends. One or two of the older women tried to catch his eye, but one look at his blank expression and they reluctantly turned away.

When his watch finally told him it was time for Katherine to leave class, he gave a hefty sigh of relief.

Quickly, he paid his bill, then rushed to the car as if he were going to a fire. In less than five minutes he was again double-parked in the same spot he had dropped Katherine off.

The large double doors opened and a flood of students poured out. It took him a moment to find Katherine in the crowd, but when he did, his brows froze into a frown. A man was walking with her, his head bent down as he tried to make a point about something or other. They stopped for a moment and let the people circle around them as he wrote something on a sheet of paper, talked to her again, then grinned broadly.

Clay could feel his temper rising to an almost combustible level. How many men did she have hanging on her string? One? Two? Fifty?

By the time she reached the car and had slipped inside, he had gotten a grip on himself. Barely.

"Who was that?" he rasped, pulling into traffic.

"My instructor." She didn't try to pretend she didn't know who he was talking about. It wasn't worth the effort.

"What was he saying?" His hands were clenched on the wheel as he turned toward the loop.

She just looked at him and his stomach lurched. "He was telling me that I could be eligible for a scholarship."

"Really? Toward what?"

"An Associate's degree. Two years of an accredited junior college education." She tried to keep her voice even, but he could hear the small thread of excitement woven in it.

"Would you like that?"

"Sure. But it's impossible to go full-time. I'll just have to do it the way I've set out: two courses at a time."

"Why?" He glanced at her, seeing the mixture of excitement and defeat and fear, all at the same time.

Her brows rose as if she thought he was just slightly touched. "Because I can't afford to go full-time."

"You could," he answered gruffly. "I'll pay for it."

He felt her body stiffen. "No, thank you. I'll manage just fine my way."

"Think about it."

"Don't try to buy me, Clay." Her hands clenched in her lap, and he had to force himself not to cover them with his own and soothe her until the tightness ebbed away.

Instead he attacked. "Isn't that what I did when I hired you as a mistress? At your own suggestion, of course."

"I wouldn't want to put you out any more than you already are," she said quietly, unwilling to voice the obvious and start another fight. It wasn't worth it.

He glanced at her, wondering if she was being sarcastic, but saw nothing in her expression to confirm it.

The silence stretched and he was afraid to break it, for the first time realizing that he wasn't the only one in pain. He'd been so deeply immersed in his own tangled emotions that he'd failed to realize just how insulting he'd become over the past few weeks. He'd heaped insult after insult on her head in an effort to keep her at a distance.

He pulled into the driveway, pushed the button that opened the garage door and drove in. They stepped out and walked into the cool, air-conditioned kitchen. It wasn't until Katherine dropped her books on the table and turned, holding on to the cane-backed chair, that he realized he'd caused what he least wanted. A confrontation.

His gut tightened at the look on her face, his hands stiffening against his sides. He would not beg. He would not let her know what that pain-filled look in her eyes was costing him.

"Ever since we met, you've accused me of being after your money. No matter what I've said or done, you've believed it."

"That's not true," he managed.

But she waved his words aside. "Yes, it is and we both know it. Every move I've made toward you, you've equated with money. Your money."

"And you've spent it."

She nodded. "Yes. When I was told to do so, I did. I was hoping you'd realize that it was you who put those boundaries on our relationship. Not me. But it didn't work."

"Are you denying that you asked to be in my bed? To live with me?" His face felt like stone, his heart like lead. He hurt both of them with his words, but it was time to air them, to let loose the doubts and thoughts that kept them emotionally apart.

"I asked for all of those things and more. I received the things—I never got what I hoped for," she said, her wide green eyes brighter with the sheen of tears that glazed them. "You see, I took a gamble. I gambled on winning the one thing I wanted the most: your love. If I'd won, I'd have won the world. If I'd lost—well, I'd have lost my own happiness. It's apparent now. All the bets are in and the race is over. I lost."

He wanted to shout at her. *No! You didn't lose! I did!* He opened his mouth, but the words refused to spill out. Instead, he sneered. "Are you telling me you'd be just as 'in love' if I was a short-order chef in a truck stop? I doubt it, Katherine."

She winced, and he pushed again, hoping she would rise to the bait and force him into accepting her on her own terms. "You like wealth just as much as the next girl, don't you? And I just happened to be at the right spot at the right time. Lucky me."

Her shoulders slumped in defeat. "Good night, Clay. We'll continue this in the morning. I think we've hurt each other enough for one day." Her body rigid, she walked out of the room toward the stairs.

Not toward his room. Not toward his bed that they'd been sharing. Not toward his arms.

As he heard the tap of her steps on the stairs, his clenched fist hit the table. "Damn!" he muttered, frustrated with his inability to cope with her home truths—and for being such an ass to begin with!

He didn't know how long he stood there, listening to her pace the bedroom above. When he finally walked toward his own room, he realized he'd been holding his breath all that time. He had prayed for her to come to him when he was at his worst, to fit herself to his body, holding him in an embrace that would allow him to cry his love and tell her of her own courage.

He took an icy cold shower more to punish himself than to eradicate his need for Katherine. His mind couldn't conceive of not having Katherine in his life, but his pride refused to allow him to go to her.

Turning the lights out, he slipped between the sheets naked and lay in the center of the bed, wishing she was there to crowd him to the side.

He hated being estranged from Katherine, but he wasn't sure what to do. Apologize? Definitely. But what else? Anything that came to mind was worth a try.

KATHERINE WAS LEERY. All morning Clay had had a smile on his face and a gleam of mischief in his eyes. Sometime during the night he'd come up with a secret that seemed to please him. She tried to recall if she'd heard the phone or the doorbell last night, but she'd heard nothing. So what had happened to make him change his attitude so quickly?

She couldn't begin to guess, and that made her even more leery.

Consuela watched them both with an eagle eye, and Katherine knew that she was wondering, too. Clay touched Katherine's shoulder every time he walked by her desk. He touched her back every time she was in the salesroom, a large room in the back with blowups of some of their most expensive properties. He smiled at her every time she turned around. It was getting on her nerves.

By five o'clock, she was ready to kill him for making her so on edge.

That morning they had driven to work together at his insistence, so she resolved to question him all the way home. When five o'clock came, she was ready. The mischief in his eyes was matched by the determination in hers.

"Ready?"

She nodded, taking her purse out of the desk drawer and standing. "Are you?"

"Oh, yes," he murmured softly, for her ears only. "Very ready."

As soon as they drove out of the lot, Katherine turned in her seat and began her line of questioning. "What's going on, Clay? All day long you've acted as if you know a secret. What is it?"

"Have I intrigued you?"

"You've angered me," she said sweetly. "Is that the same thing?"

His chuckle reverberated through the Porsche's interior. "Not quite," he said finally. "But give me an hour or so and I'll see if I can't change your mind."

Katherine sat back, her arms crossed over her seat belt. She'd be *damned* if she'd voice any curiosity!

They drove through the usual afternoon traffic, but instead of aiming for home, Clay took the freeway to the Austin cutoff.

He glanced in her direction. "Aren't you going to ask me where we're going?"

"No."

He shrugged and picked up the sleek car phone that sat between the bucket seats. A few moments of cryptic conversation and they were pulling up in front of a well-known Italian restaurant. Clay drove around the back and gave two short honks. The chef, with profuse movements and even more profuse chuckles, set a large Styrofoam basket in the deep trunk. Then they drove away.

This time her curiosity couldn't be quelled. "What is it?" she asked, determined to get an answer.

"Dinner."

"Thanks for the explanation." She leaned back, surveying the roadside. The tantalizing aroma of pasta in rich sauce, garlic and other spices wafted through the interior. She tried to ignore it, but her stomach wouldn't cooperate; it growled daintily.

Clay glanced at his watch. "Good. We'll be there in time for sunset."

"Oh, wonderful," she cooed. "Then we have time to hide from vampires."

His brows arched. "Vampires? Aren't you being a little dramatic?"

"Aren't you?" she countered and was pleased to note his slight blush.

Another phone call and fifteen minutes later, Clay parked the car on a wide gravel driveway in front of a rustic log cabin. At least she assumed it was supposed to be a cabin, though to her it looked like a huge ranch house.

Just beyond the house she could see a trail leading through trees and sloping down to a dock where a cabin cruiser bobbed gently in the water. Katherine had seen the signs heralding Canyon Lake, but she hadn't really believed they were headed there. She'd been wrong. Clay had surprised her again.

He turned off the engine and stepped out of the car, pocketing the keys. Katherine stayed seated. "Coming?"

"Anywhere in particular?"

"We're here."

He reached in the trunk and pulled out the cooler and she had no choice but to follow. Her stomach was growling and it was no longer a dainty sound. "Are we renting a rowboat?"

"Something like that," he said, walking past the house and down toward the dock, careful to match his longer strides to her shorter ones.

"Is this place yours?" she asked, stepping carefully so that her heels wouldn't get caught in the spaces between the boards. It was silly to ask, but she didn't know what else to say.

"Of course," he answered, apparently surprised at her question. "Why?"

"I just wondered." She shrugged as he stepped onto what looked like an ocean cruiser to her. He set down the Styrofoam container and held his hand out to help her aboard. "Several of my friends have cabin cruisers," she said, "but theirs float in tubs."

His chuckle was delicious, sending shivers down her spine. So did his touch. His hand was warm and comforting and...sexy. His thumb rubbed against her palm and her body reacted immediately. Her breath shortened. Her muscles tightened.

"It's beautiful," she said, deliberately ignoring him as she looked around the deck. Lights flowed up from the downstairs of the cabin, shedding a pale glow on the pilot house. The sun was just getting ready to set and the sky was shot with pink and blue.

Everything on the boat was either sparkling white or deep gray, and in tip-top condition.

"I like it, but I don't get much of a chance to use it."

"Why?"

"Business keeps getting in the way."

"It seems to me you could conduct your business just as well here as over a restaurant table. In fact, it'd be more relaxing for some of your clients."

"I'd need a hostess to help me with the details."

"Like Magda?" Her voice was sweet, but the venom of the thought was just underneath the surface.

"Don't start, Katherine," he warned, for the first time all day, his frown appeared. "This is our time, let's not ruin it."

She had the grace to flush. He was right. This wasn't the time for a confrontation. A lethargy assailed her. She wanted peace from all the hassling of the past weeks. She needed time to just sit and stare at the sunset and speak nonsense. So much had happened to her that her energies were still running at full speed, while her mind was as tired as a two-year-old looking for a place to nap. Perhaps he would broach the subject of his canceled engagement and what her role in his life was supposed to be. Perhaps . . .

"Champagne?" He held a fluted tulip glass in front of her, his eyes silently asking her to just *be* with him.

She couldn't refuse. "I'd love it," she murmured, accepting the glass and giving a slight salute before sipping the bubbly liquid.

"Come sit." He led her to two gray-and-white-striped, padded chaise longues under the full back canopy.

Slipping off her shoes, she gave a sigh and began to sink to the cushions, but his hand still holding hers gave a tug. "Not there. Here," he said and pulled her onto his lap.

She barely kept the glass from spilling. "Cozy."

"Exactly the way I planned it."

She tipped her head back and smiled, snuggling against him. She heard his quick intake of breath. "Then why put out two chairs?"

"I didn't." He kissed the tip of her nose, his expression purposely bland. Not yet. Not yet. Every woman needed romance in her life.... "I asked Drake to ready the boat for guests. This was his doing."

"Who's Drake?"

"He lives two houses over and helps keep an eye on the property for me."

She sighed again, loving the feel of his free hand as it roamed up and down her arm. The sun played across the water, making red and black shadows dance for them. The peace invaded her. Water slapping softly against the side of the boat and an occasional bird call were the only sounds. Ever so slowly, darkness descended.

"Comfortable?" he murmured in her ear.

"Perfect," she said, wiggling her bottom against the seat. And against his side.

"Then stop that or we'll be exercising before we've eaten."

Her giggle filled the air, but the tense excitement that had been blossoming ever since they stepped aboard was heightened. His arm tightened around her, and she leaned into the strength of his body, loving the feel of him surrounding her. He was everything she could ever want in a man. Everything except that he refused to declare his love.... Stop! her mind cautioned. Not today. Not this moment. Later. Later.

When he kissed her, she melted into him. His hand reached and found the glass of champagne and made it disappear. She didn't care. He was intoxicating enough for her. Her hands couldn't stay still. Instead they strayed across his chest as she turned into his arms. Her fingers played with the buttons of his shirt, undoing them one by one. She wanted to feel his skin, to smell the scent of him, to rest her cheek against the strength of his heartbeat.

She felt rather than heard her dress zipper slide down. The cool breeze touched her skin at the same time as the warmth of his hand traced her back. "Mmm, you feel wonderful. So sleek and soft in all the right places," he said hoarsely.

She kissed his chest. "So are you."

"I hope not," he chuckled, and she blushed.

"I didn't say soft in the wrong places," she corrected, laying her hand lightly on his hardened desire.

And then she was sitting alone. He stood next to her, his hand outstretched. "Come on," he said.

"Where to?" She was dizzy with the need for him, and confused that he would leave her.

"Below. I don't want anybody with binoculars watching us."

10

HE PULLED HER into his embrace, giving her a light squeeze before leading her by the hand to the steep stairs that took them below. Vaguely she registered the living area, a small galley and a booth with a built-in dining table, but it was the last room that stunned her. The bedroom. It was larger than she could have thought possible, and a king-size bed dominated the room. Built-in dressers, a closet and side tables with lamps and books stacked haphazardly made up the rest of the furnishings. She reached out and stroked her hand over the spread; it was a dark fur that felt as luxurious as it looked.

Katherine glanced over her shoulder. Clay stood just behind her, his shirt undone, his tie hanging on either side of his collar. His eyes were ablaze, and his thoughts were transmitted to her as easily as radio signals.

With slow, studied movements, she let her dress fall in a puddle to the floor. She slipped the straps of her teddy off her shoulders and allowed it to follow the dress.

Clay groaned, and without another sound he shed his own clothes, then took her in his arms, kissing her as if there were no other way to communicate.

When he pressed her back against the fur, she went willingly. Her heart was beating so quickly it sounded like a trip-hammer in her ears. "Clay, I—" she began, but his firm lips stopped her.

"Shh," he murmured against her partially opened mouth. "Later. Everything can wait until later."

They kissed without reservation, their arms and legs and souls entwined in that inner space that makes two people one. Their movements matched perfectly, bringing pleasure to both. And their senses were so highly tuned to each other that they flowed together like the lapping waves outside. He coaxed her with his body and hands and tongue and she reacted with emotions and feelings she had never felt before. Then she lost herself in him.

Her last thought before shattering into a thousand pieces was that he *had* to love her. No one could do this to her, make her feel this way without that special ingredient.

Later that night, dressed in nothing but a teddy and the diamond and emerald earrings, Katherine sat cross-legged on the bed and grinned at Clay. He'd donned his dark blue, tight-fitting underwear, but that was all. His broad chest, well-developed arms and a smile was all he needed.

"What are you grinning about?" he asked, holding out a piece of hot garlic bread for her to taste.

She took a bite, then chewed and swallowed before answering. "How adorable you are."

His brows rose. "I've been called a lot things, but never that."

"That's because you've never let yourself relax before."

"I haven't had the time until recently." He swirled his fork in the mound of spaghetti in front of him and opened his mouth.

"You had the time," she corrected softly. "You just weren't willing to take it."

His eyes pinned her, looking deep into her soul. "Maybe," he hedged.

Her heart sank just a little. When would he learn to be unguarded with her? To be natural all the time instead of just those few moments when his actions loudly spoke the words he wasn't willing to say. He was so guarded.

"Maybe I didn't know how to relax until recently." He dropped his gaze and moved the plate to the nightstand.

"Did you know that on occasion people have *combined* business and pleasure? And very successfully, too, I hear."

He laughed. "Are you suggesting I try it?"

"Why not?" she asked before taking another bite of garlic bread.

"Why not, indeed," he repeated, sweeping away the rest of the dishes and reaching for her. "It's certainly something to think about." He pulled her with him to stretch out on the bed, molding her to his form and sighing deeply. "Some other time."

Pitching the bread after the spaghetti plate, she tried to stifle the yawn that worked its way out, but couldn't.

"Sleep, sweetheart," he murmured into her hair. And she did.

TWO HOURS LATER, when she awoke, Clay was still there. Next to her. She edged closer and he moved, seeking the curves of her waist and hip, his fingers trailing lightly across her skin.

"You feel so delicate, so exquisite." His voice in her ear, husky with sleep, did crazy things to her libido. But making love wasn't all they could do.

She pulled away and undid each earring, setting them side by side on the nightstand closest to her. Clay watched greedily as her hands moved gracefully. He was entranced. As he tried to grasp her, Katherine slipped off the bed and unsnapped her teddy as she danced away. "I think you need to cool off, Mr. Reynolds," she teased throatily just before disappearing through the door.

Clay jumped up and followed, a chuckle caught in his throat. Would he ever be able to second-guess her? By the time he reached the deck, Katherine was poised on the edge of the boat, heart-stoppingly naked and in a perfect diving position. Her head was tilted toward him, twinkling eyes teasing. Taunting.

He crossed his arms and leaned against the bulkhead, still feasting his senses. "Don't you think it might be wise to check the depth before diving?"

"I already did."

"When?"

"When we came on board I saw the post in the water. The water mark says twelve feet."

He grinned. "How perceptive."

"Aren't I, though." And then she disappeared, cutting cleanly through the air and into the water. Clay walked to the side and waited, his eyes scanning the lightly rippled surface for her.

When she appeared just five or six feet from the boat she looked like a sleek mermaid. Her smile was diamonds on black velvet, her skin translucent. "Come in," she called.

"Come out," he countered, and as she trod water they gazed at each other, both knowing the hunger was building to impossible heights. It curled in his groin and snaked through his blood. He needed her.

Without another thought, he dived in. Before he surfaced, he encountered her flesh, and his arms went around her waist as he broke from the water.

"Are you real?" she asked breathlessly, stroking his hair from his eyes before resting her hands on his shoulders.

"Very real." He pulled her closer, their legs entwined. "Feel me."

Then his lips captured hers and the water swirled around them as they sank into the moon-drenched water. For a fleeting moment Clay thought that Katherine brought stars with her wherever she was; on the boat—or below the shimmering surface of the water.

IT WASN'T UNTIL early morning that Clay realized just how wonderful this respite had been. His original plan had been to soften her up so she wouldn't be so angry with him when he finally confessed his broken engagement. He'd forgotten all about his confession.

She had taught him a few things instead. Her openness and charm had seeped into his very soul, but it was that same openness that scared the hell out of him. He made coffee with automatic movements, his mind consumed with the woman curled so enticingly in his bed.

He wanted to go slow and make sure this wasn't a fleeting form of happiness that would wear off and leave them both with sour tastes in their mouths. He wanted to move with caution as they entered this new phase of their relationship.

But what he really wanted was a guarantee that this would build into a lasting relationship, one that they would both be happy to share for the rest of their lives. Only there was no such an animal.

But he could try. In several months—perhaps a year—he'd know if this liaison was real or a mistake. Then—and only then—he'd ask her to marry him.

"Mmm," Katherine said as she walked into the room running her fingers through her riot of curls. She'd slipped into one of his old T-shirts. He could almost see the small scraps of lace she called panties.... "Coffee always smells more delicious than it tastes. Best smell in the world to wake up to." Her arms wrapped around his waist and she gave a hug before pulling away and reaching for a cup.

"You've got another hour before we have to get ready to leave. Why don't you go back to bed?"

She shook her head. "I want to see the sunrise and that should be taking place in another fifteen minutes or so."

"Sunrise?" He looked blank.

"Of course. It's when the sun comes up and brightens the day?"

"I know what it is. Why?"

"Because it's beautiful." Her voice was soft, her green eyes luminous.

She poured each of them a cup of coffee and they sat in the small plush booth and stared out the window, watching the dark of night slowly lighten to a dim gray.

This was peace. Once more he experienced that deep feeling of contentment. He'd known the pride of succeeding, the ups and downs of happiness and depression. But contentment was different. It had everything to do with the woman who sat next to him, her eyes bright with wonder and light.

"I love you." His voice was low and slow and meltingly soft.

She turned her head slowly, a stunned expression on her face. "Say that again."

"No. Once was enough." He smiled, his finger tilting her chin up so her lips were accessible to his. "But it's true."

"What does it mean?" she whispered.

His lips grazed hers. "It means shut up and kiss me."

And she did, until a loud voice caused them to jump apart.

"Hello! Anyone aboard?"

"Damn!" Clay muttered.

"Who is it?"

"Drake. As usual his timing is off." Clay stood and walked to the steps. "Down here, Drake, and you'd better have a damn good excuse for being the early bird."

"I do," the deep voice boomed. "Or I wouldn't bother with the likes of you."

The man who came down the stairs and shook hands with Clay was enormous, taking up practically all the available breathing space. Brilliant blue eyes highlighted a face covered with a dark beard and mustache.

"And how are your corn and green beans growing?" Katherine couldn't help asking. He wasn't green, but he was certainly a jolly giant.

His chuckle reverberated through the boat. "Just fine, thank you. I'm having a problem with my rutabagas, but Little Sprout seems to have a green thumb." His eyes twinkled as he scanned her small form perched on the booth seat. "Are you a little friend of his?"

She grinned. "Believe it or not, I'm a full grown person."

"What's the problem, Drake?" Clay broke in, apparently not liking the tone of the conversation. He hadn't even introduced them and they were cracking jokes.

Drake grabbed a cup and poured himself some coffee, then sat across from Katherine. Clay slid in beside her, his arm proprietarily across the back of the seat.

"Well, your engine is coughing. I think you might need an overhaul." He raised his dark brows. "Remember I told you last year that the carburetor and the fuel pump were both acting up?"

"I remember. Who do you recommend?"

The large man shrugged. "I've got one or two names in mind. I thought you might want them to bid on the job. Want me to find out and let you know?"

Clay nodded. "How long will the boat be out of commission?"

"Two weeks. Maybe three."

"Good enough." Clay stood, pointedly staring down at his neighbor. "We've got to get dressed and head back. Thanks for your help and advice."

Drake looked at his still-full cup and sighed regretfully, getting Clay's message. "And thanks for the delicious cup of coffee."

He stood and Katherine stretched her hand across the table. "It was good to meet you, Drake."

His clasp was warm and gentle, his eyes admiring. "You're one little fish I wouldn't throw back," he said, sliding a glance sideways to Clay.

"Drake," Clay warned, and the giant withdrew his hand.

"She's a keeper. Mind your manners," he muttered to Clay, and Katherine had to hold in a grin. Clay obviously couldn't see the funny side of his behavior.

Clay sat back down, slumping against the cushions. "Damn that man."

"Why?"

"Because he always tries to force me into decisions I'm not ready to make yet."

"The engine?" Katherine said, misunderstanding. "But he said it was acting up long before this."

Clay relaxed. She obviously didn't realize that his neighbor had been making a move on her. Drake was a ladies' man who played everything slow and easy, but got what he wanted every time. "You're right," he murmured, taking her back into his arms. His lips grazed hers. "Now where were we?"

"We were getting ready to go to work. Remember?"

He closed his eyes and groaned. "Right. Work." He opened one eye and looked down at her. "You wouldn't consider playing hookey, would you? I don't think the boss would mind."

Her hand trailed his jaw, but there was regret in her green eyes. "No, but the boss's secretary would be livid. She has a doctor's appointment this morning and there'd be no one there to cover the phone."

Clay kissed the tip of her nose. "You're off the hook for now, Katherine, but I won't forget where we left off."

"Neither will I, Clay," she promised, giving him a quick hug before formally ending the most wonderful night of her life.

When it was time to leave, Clay took one more quick tour around the interior, making sure everything was turned off and locked up. He glanced around the bedroom, spying the earrings that lay on the far nightstand. Picking them up, he remembered in his mind's eye how she'd looked last night dressed in nothing but those two pieces of jewelry, her skin translucent, her eyes filled with green fire. He had never felt so connected to anyone before!

He pocketed the earrings and finished closing up the boat. Later tonight, he decided, he'd give her back her inheritance. The earrings belonged to her and always would. Katherine and the earrings were inseparable.

THE DAY DRAGGED. Clay had a full calendar, but his mind was on a boat on Canyon Lake with a red-haired witch who had placed him under her spell.

And while one part of him wanted to hold her to him, the other part was scared to death of the commitment she represented. Never had he had his emotions in such turmoil, and that turmoil seemed to produce nothing but more chaos.

He kept telling himself that he suffered from that old fight-or-flight syndrome. And he wasn't sure which he was supposed to do. Drawn to her, he was also afraid of her. She was so strong and capable and honest. He'd never met anyone like her before. But would marriage turn her into the tyrant he'd known other women to be? Would she be bitter when business interfered? Would she pout when he couldn't give her her way when she wanted it? How much change would she undergo after a wedding ring was placed on her finger?

Time. He needed time to absorb it all and then he'd know the right thing to do.

When the workday finally came to a close, he gave a sigh of relief. He'd changed most of his appointments so that he could leave with Katherine. He'd even canceled a dinner he was supposed to attend. He wanted—craved—time with her.

He loved her. He'd said so. Once. That had to count for something.

"CLAY?"

"Mmm?" he asked, maneuvering through the afternoon traffic toward home.

"Where are we going?"

"Home. Did you want to go somewhere else?"

"No, I mean—where are *we* going? Are we going to continue to drift in this relationship or will it change into something else? What?"

He pulled into the garage and shut off the engine. "I don't know." It was too soon for this. Too soon. "What were you expecting, Katherine?"

"I don't know." She opened her door and stepped out, going directly into the kitchen, refusing to look at him. Surely he could see that she was perfect for him! How stubborn could the man get? "I just know that I want to be with you forever, but you seem content to let us drift along with no sense of beginning or end."

"Is this a proposal?" He hadn't meant for his voice to be so hard, but she was pushing. He could feel his adrenaline pumping. Fight or flight. He began defrosting chicken breasts in the microwave, his attaché case still on the kitchen table.

"No." Her voice was stilted, stiff. She picked up a head of lettuce and showered it with water.

"What exactly do you want me to say, Katherine?" He turned on the broiler and readied a shallow pan. His movements were quick, decisive. Not at all like his brain. Damn! She was stubborn!

"I want—need—some kind of commitment. Obviously you aren't ready for that." She broke the lettuce into bite-size pieces.

When the breasts were in the broiler, he began slicing fresh tomatoes and small yellow squash. "You're right. I'm not ready. And neither are you."

"Don't speak for me, Clay. I know what I am and what I'm not." She set the table.

"You don't know a damn thing, girl. You're still living in some dream world where the fairy princess meets and falls in love with the prince and they live happily ever after! That's not real life." She dumped the lettuce in a large bowl as he reached for the salad tongs. While he tossed the salad, she sprinkled in the dressing.

"I know the difference, Clay. Believe me, you wouldn't fit into a suit of armor!" She put the salad on the table with a bang.

"And you're no princess!" Clay took the breasts out of the broiler and set them on the plate.

Dinner was a silent affair.

As a matter of fact, the rest of the evening was a war of silence. Clay lay in his own bed, listening to Katherine's footsteps as she paced the upstairs room, where she'd chosen to sleep.

Damn her! All she had to do was give him some time to sort this out.

He heard her footsteps on the stairs and he stilled. The footsteps came closer.

"Clay?"

Her soft voice melted away the anger and the indecision. She was right and he'd been wrong. He loved her. He'd loved her ever since he'd met her—he just hadn't wanted to admit it. Well, now was the time to make a commitment, but he was leery. She'd understand. He smiled, grateful that she had been adult enough to come to him.

Flipping on the side light, he sat up and watched as she walked into the room. A brilliant red T-shirt proclaimed it was good to hug a teddy, which brought to mind the black one he would always remember. Instead of the color clashing with her riot of curls, it turned them golden. He could feel himself grow and harden with desire for her.

"I need you to sign this," she said softly, holding out the papers clutched in her hand. Laura had given her the outline of a contract for her services and she hoped—prayed—that this would be the impetus to make Clay realize that they belonged together. In marriage.

"What is it?"

She took a deep breath, willing herself to be calm. "It's a rough draft of a contract that states when either of us is ready to end our relationship, I'll get a small settlement and won't sue. It also stipulates that you'll pay my clothing bills and a few other incidentals."

"We're going to build a contract?" His eyes scanned the sheets, turning icier with every word. He looked up, pinning her feet to the floor, his almost overwhelming anger plain to see. "What are the terms?"

"First of all, that I have a set of keys to your home."

"Agreed."

"That I also have a set of keys to both cars."

"Agreed." His eyes were still flinty. Her heart sank. He wasn't warming up to this idea at all.

She barged ahead. "That you agree to help me in any way necessary while I go for my college degree."

"Agreed."

"Every Sunday we go out for dinner. My choice of restaurant, and no combining business with pleasure on that day."

A muscle twitched at his mouth, and she prayed it wasn't the beginning of a temper tantrum. This was hard enough. "What if I don't like your choice?"

"I won't choose food you can't eat, Clay," she admonished sternly. "But I want to be well treated. Mistresses have their price."

"So do misters."

"What?"

"Never mind. What else?"

"You have to supply me with two weeks' notice and severance pay if you decide you want to terminate our relationship."

"A two week notice?" His voice was a roar.

She nodded. Had she gone too far? Could Laura have been wrong in assuming that this would make Clay realize what he and Katherine had?

"Severance pay?" He roared again.

She nodded again, her heartbeat pounding in her ears.

"What the hell are you planning to do with this money? Open a business?"

So he was already thinking of the end of their relationship. Tears prickled in her eyes, but she refused to let them fall. Later, she told herself. Later, when she was alone. "No. I just have to look out for myself."

"Yourself?" His tone was derisive enough to tear at her soul like a knife.

Her chin lifted stubbornly. "I may need to look for another benefactor."

Those words were tinder to the fire. Fury blazed in his eyes and she took a step away. Then his fury turned to a cold wariness she hadn't seen before. Would she never understand what to expect from him next? When he finally spoke, his voice was low and under control again. Barely. "You say you love me, then ask me to sign this document. You don't love me enough to trust me to take care of you?"

"You've only said the words once, Clay, and I'm supposed to be happy and reassured by that? With your obvious reluctance to even mouth the words I need to hear, you expect me to believe you'll take care of me? Won't that cramp your style with your new wife?"

Clay ran a hand through his hair. "Look," he said, patting the mattress beside him. "Come sit down and let me explain this."

"What?" Her smile was brittle. "That you broke up with Magda weeks ago, but didn't have the courtesy to tell me? Even after the most tender, wonderful, intimate night on your boat? How will you explain that you'd have me carry the guilt of taking another woman's man rather than live with being defenseless against a five-foot ogre with a G.E.D. for a high school diploma?"

His eyes narrowed. "You knew?"

She nodded. "I knew. Otherwise I wouldn't be here."

"Then why the contract? Why can't we just continue the way we are? As friends?"

"Because this isn't friendship!" *This is love* her heart cried. "Please read it."

"You aren't serious!"

Frustration warred with anger. "Why not? Why is it all right for you to draw up contracts with everyone you do business with, and it's not all right for me to do so?"

"Our relationship isn't business!"

"Then what is it? A living arrangement? Even renters sign leases!"

"This is sex! You set the rules yourself!"

Her eyes widened with the pain of his words. She closed them, praying for the strength to carry this argument to a conclusion and get out of here as quickly as possible. She didn't know how much longer her shaking legs would hold her. "Is it, Clay?" she asked. "Is that what this is all about? Sex?"

He balled the papers in his hand and threw them on the floor. "Dammit! You're trying to force me into making a decision that I'm not ready to make! And I

won't sign a contract for that! You can consider this a
two-week notice!"

Her tears were replaced by anger. Full-blown anger.
"Great!" she cried around the lump in her throat. "Now
I understand. The fine print doesn't have to be magni-
fied for me to get the meaning." She pivoted, heading
through the bedroom door.

"Where in hell do you think you're going?"

"To bed. *My* bed. This is one of my two nights off per
week. Read the contract."

"I didn't sign the damn thing so it's not legal, you little idiot!"

"I'm abiding by it, anyway," she threw over her
shoulder just seconds before slamming his door with a
resounding bang.

He unclenched his hands and covered his face. What
the hell had he just done?

A small voice laughed at him. He'd just chased off the
woman he loved. He'd played the ass so beautifully he
deserved an Academy Award. Clay Reynolds, who had
always been in control, just lost it.

He had wanted her to come to him in love, because
she couldn't do without him. He wanted her willing and
warm and begging for his affection so he wouldn't have
to show just how much he cared. He wanted her to give
so he wouldn't have to. He wanted to cut his throat with
a dull razor for being the stupid fool that he was.

It was early morning before he finally fell asleep. His
last thought was that he had played the witless fool long
enough. Tomorrow he would shove his pride aside and
ask for her forgiveness. Perhaps, if he were lucky, he'd
be able to admit just how stupid he'd grown in his adult
life. And then he'd marry her so she couldn't pull a stunt
like this again.

KATHERINE SLIPPED soundlessly out the door and into the dark early-morning coolness. The Lincoln sat directly in front, and she slid into the driver's seat.

Once she had decided on a course of action, she had packed quickly and efficiently, taking just what she needed for the next week or so and leaving the rest in paper bags next to the door. They'd be out of Clay's way and ready to pick up once she decided on her next step.

Before leaving, though, she had deposited a letter directly on top of the answering machine in his study, knowing he would check it in the morning since he hadn't done so last night.

She had pushed Clay too hard by asking him to sign that stupid contract. Instead of him laughing at it, he'd taken it seriously, losing his temper and dismissing her from his life. She would have given anything to retract that move, but it was too late. Too late for both of them.

She'd lost Clay, either because she wasn't right for him or because he just didn't care for her enough. She had always thought it was the former, but now she realized it was the latter. Either way, the results were the same.

And she couldn't stand the thought of staying and conducting a postmortem on their dead relationship, which would certainly have happened this morning. Apparently he was right. After bedding her, he was sated and ready to move on. Clay would have continued keeping that distance-serving wall up, and she would have become more hurt by banging her head against it.

No, this was the only way to end their relationship. Anything else would be more harmful to her, and she didn't think she could handle that. Her emotions were already too tattered.

He'd tried to buy her without the benefit of marriage, never seeing that she bled every time he offered his bribes, was wounded every time he denied her gift of love.

She parked the car at the curb and walked up the steps to Laura's front door. All she wanted was her own room and a good cry. And not necessarily in that order....

11

CLAY SAT straight up in bed, his body slick with sweat. His gaze darted to the pillow next to him, then bounced around the room. Taking short, panting breathes, he tried to control his breathing. He'd had a nightmare about Katherine.

He slipped his feet off the side of the bed and strode naked toward her room. She had to be there. She had to be!

Her room was as neat as when she had first walked in. The closets were open to show they were empty, the bed made without a crease. Three paper bags of clothing stood by the door, the only remains of her visit. Visit. That was the key word. He'd treated her like a visitor and everyone else like old friends. But he hadn't been afraid of everyone else—just Katherine.

She had petrified him.

He now knew the whole contract thing had been staged as a joke to shake him out of his complacency with their relationship. Juvenile, but a joke, nonetheless. If he'd only treated it as such instead of allowing his anger to get the best of him, Katherine would still be with him right now. Instead, he'd fought her because he'd felt as if he was being backed into a corner.

She'd wanted a commitment as grand as her love for him, and he'd been reluctant to verbalize one. It wasn't a bad request. In fact, asking for him to love her in return was only honest. Just as she was.

He dropped to the edge of her bed, his head in his hands, as despair washed over him. He had been blind and stupid and now he was about to pay for the pain he knew he had caused her. She wasn't like any other woman he had known. She wasn't like his mother, and he wasn't like his father.

He'd seen his father die a little every time he'd been tongue-lashed by his mother. He'd seen his mother turn into a bitter woman because his father couldn't—or wouldn't—live up to his grand talk. Both had been vulnerable to love and neither had won. So they'd spent the rest of their lives together and miserable.

Clay had grown up an only child and just as frustrated as his parents. He'd spent most of his time away from the house, visiting David's family because he couldn't stand his own parents' constant bickering.

Then, over the years he began noticing that David's parents did the same thing. David's father was a mechanic who never had enough money to support six kids. And David's mother was unhappy working her life away as a civilian secretary at one of the air bases.

Then there was Laura. Her parents were wealthy and, though they never got along, money had allowed them to keep the necessary distance so they could at least be civil to each other....

But for the first time in his life it dawned on him that if any of their parents had ever separated they'd probably still have been miserable. One fed off the other, and each in his own way got something out of their bizarre relationships. Otherwise, they wouldn't have remained in them.

And Clay had thought he'd been so smart, refraining from anything that smacked of vulnerability when it came to females. He'd tried and discarded women like cheap pairs of pants, not really believing any of them were more emotionally involved than he was.

How many people had he hurt the way Katherine was hurting him? He was afraid to guess, but the idea wasn't at all pleasant. Now he was going to find out about hurt himself. Firsthand.

He had to explain to her, see her. He had to make her understand that he had been scared to death of everything she'd made him feel. That he'd built walls to defend himself against the emotions she evoked in him. And he'd done such a damn fine job of it, he had walled himself in and shut love out.

Filled with purpose, he stood. She must have gone to Laura's. Where else could she go? He'd confront her with what he'd learned about himself. She'd understand, he knew it. Then they'd get married. It was as right for them now as it would be a year from now. So why wait?

It was so simple that he smiled. Everything would work out....

IT TOOK KATHERINE an hour to stop the tears that felt as if they were being dredged up from her very soul. But finally she sat up from her bed in Laura's house and determinedly began to formulate plans.

She couldn't stay here. Clay would immediately guess where she was, and she'd have to go through the post mortem of their parting. She wasn't strong enough for that—not yet....

Picking up the phone, she dialed the only person she could trust besides Laura.

"Consuela? I have a favor to ask," she began.

CLAY BANGED on Laura's front door, impatience edging his voice as he called out. "Katherine! Open up! I know you're in there!"

There was no answer.

Only after minutes of knocking did he remember that Laura always kept a key in the fern plant hanging over the front balcony. Reaching in, he patted the dirt until he founded what he was seeking. With a sigh of relief, he unlocked the door and strode in, searching each room as he made his way to Katherine's. But when he reached the room, his footsteps halted and his heart thudded with fear.

The dresser was empty of cosmetics, the closet void of shoes. Everything was gone.

She was gone.

Where? Where could she go? Laura was the only friend he knew about, but apparently there were others.

Her brother? No, she wouldn't return to a job she hated, no matter how close she was to her brother. David? He wouldn't dare. Where? He pulled a blank.

Cursing under his breath, he called himself the biggest fool of all. He'd gotten what he deserved and it tasted like bile on his tongue.

He'd find her. He swore he would. And when he did, he'd hold her so tight she'd never be able to run again. Ever.

Turning, he strode from the house and jumped into his car. Maybe, just maybe, he'd drive up to the office and she'd be there, working away as usual.

He prayed so, but somehow he knew he was living in a fantasy world. The same one he'd been living in for thirty-odd years.

HE CRIED when he found her note later that evening.

> Dear Clay,
> I won't be your personal whipping boy. I've done
> nothing except love you and that isn't a big enough
> crime to be punished for. I hope you find what-
> ever it is you're seeking.

For the rest of the week, Clay scoured San Antonio.
He figured it wouldn't be too hard to find her. There
weren't that many redheads in the Spanish-textured
city. There probably weren't that many in the whole
darned state. Or the country, for that matter. At least
not natural ones with long bouncing curls that dared a
man to tangle his fingers in the sweet luxury of it.

No one had seen her.

He'd even gone to San Antonio College and checked
with her math professor. With a rigid nod and as few
words as possible, the man had coldly informed him
that Katherine had dropped out of school. Obviously
he blamed Clay.

So did Clay.

Unending frustration and a terrifying depth of loneliness were now his constant companions. Everything
he did or said emphasized just how many mistakes he
had made in his personal life. He didn't even have any
friends to turn to anymore, and his family. . . Well, his
family would remain at a distance. At his wish. There
were still too many bad tasting memories of his youth
for him to turn to them now.

Shortly after her leaving, Clay had sat in the living
room and listened to Katherine's favorite country-and-
western station while staring at the jewels that would
forever link him to her. Turning on the lamp next to

him, he squinted to see the engraving on the backs of the earrings.

He could make out the crest, but time had worn the edges away. Several lines, obviously representing mountains, were on the left side of the shield while three stars formed a triangle on the right. Impatience made him mutter as he stalked to his desk and rummaged through the drawers until he found what he was looking for: a magnifying glass.

With the glass he could see the name Montclair just below the crest. He carefully placed that earring on the table and picked up the other one. Just as Katherine had said, there were initials and an inscription: A., *avec amour*, C.

So they had been given with love.

He didn't know the past history of these gems, but he was smart enough to realize that Katherine's parents had had a love just as strong as the original owners. A love that made all else trivial compared to that emotion.

He placed the earring next to its mate and dropped the magnifying glass on the sofa.

Katherine. Katherine. Katherine. His pulse thrummed the name in his ears. He loved her with all his heart and soul and he had never trusted her with his love enough to give it to her as a gift. No strings attached, just love.

He had to find her, to explain. She was everything to him. There would never be anyone else in his life who would make him face himself this way or help him to find happiness.

Katherine. Katherine. Katherine.

Picking the earrings up once more and holding them tight in his hands, he bent his head.

Whoever had been given the earrings first had been loved. And Katherine had received them in love, too.

Then she had given them to him.

He remembered Katherine sitting in his car as she placed the jewels carefully in his palm. He should have known then. She had faced and accepted her love for him, and he hadn't had the ability to see it.

He hadn't had the ability to love, either. But Katherine had been patient with him, teaching him what love was and that he was truly capable of that emotion. She had taught him the most important lesson he would ever learn.

He prayed it wasn't too late to show her just how much he loved her.

At work, Consuela's all-knowing eyes kept condemning him, and for once he accepted that burden. She'd known from the first that Katherine wouldn't return to work. She'd even had a sixth sense concerning Clay's relationship with Katherine. And how much of an ass he'd been. There was nothing she could accuse him of that he hadn't already blamed himself for a thousand times over. It was a tough road that led adolescence to emotional adulthood—especially at the age of thirty-five.

But the one person he leaned on the hardest was Laura. She knew something, he was sure. She had to. She and Katherine had become best of friends, and neither Laura's relationship with David nor Katherine's with him had interfered.

For the fourth time in a week he tracked her down at David's home one evening. It was immediately apparent that they had come to an agreement, and love was once more in bloom. Clay tamped down his flaring envy as he watched the glances between them that spoke of an honest and true love. He finally believed in that commodity. It was a shame he'd learned so late.

"Have you heard from her at all?" Clay asked, his eyes pleading more than his words.

Reluctantly, Laura nodded her head. "But I—"

"I know," he interrupted tiredly. "You won't tell me where she is."

"Right."

"Is she all right?"

"She's fine."

"She hasn't gone back to her brother, has she? I don't think I could take it if I scared her back into that jerk's house."

"No." Laura chuckled. "I'd hog-tie her myself before she did something that stupid." The smile slipped from her face. "But your brain cells haven't worked very well so far, Clay," she admonished.

"Laura . . ." David warned.

But Clay waved a dismissive hand in the air. "No, David. She's right. I've been acting like a male pig all these years. Then when I finally meet the woman I want to share my life with, I force her into battle at every turn. I wanted her to prove herself worthy of me when I wasn't good enough for her." He leaned back, closing his eyes for a moment. Anguish, never completely gone, flooded him again. "Ironic, isn't it?"

"Sad." Laura's hand covered his on the table. "You've never spent much time on relationships before, have you, Clay?"

He shook his head, absently wondering where his words were pouring from now. He'd never opened up to anyone before, except to Katherine. "Every spark of energy I had went to business. I'm good at that," he said derisively. "But I can't seem to show the woman I love that I need her more than breath. It's hard to do when I keep breathing anyway."

He earned a chuckle from both David and Laura, but in his heart he knew he was right. He knew nothing about personal relationships and their intricate workings.

But David knew. "Did you goad her like you used to push the rest of us, making us prove ourselves until we told you we liked you even when you were a bas—" he glanced at Laura "—a stinker?"

Clay nodded. There was no use denying it.

"Then you deserve what you got," David said, his voice hard. "Take the time to look at yourself, man. You had this coming. You haven't made a new friend—personal friend—since college. You've been a loner for as long as I can remember. And your ideas about women were already well fed before then. It wasn't without justification, Clay, but you're smart enough to know that all kettles aren't black."

Standing, Clay clenched his hands in his pockets. "I'm well aware of my own shortcomings, or I wouldn't be here begging for help." His voice was low and harsh. "But none of us was raised without hang-ups of some kind. This one happened to be mine."

He stood and glanced at Laura, making certain David understood that he was referring to David's own hang-up about Laura and the fact that even when she returned, David had refused to seek her out. Laura had practically had to attack him just to get noticed. "We're all learning."

"Touché," David said softly as he watched his best friend walk from the room.

"You deserved that," Laura whispered in his ear, giving him a light kiss while she was at it.

"I know. I just didn't think he'd retaliate. He's been down so long that I didn't think he'd rise above it."

"Never underestimate our Clay, honey. He's had a tough lesson to learn, but it wasn't all his fault. Our fair sex had more than a little to do with it. His mother in particular."

David hugged her closely. "I'm glad to hear you admit it. It's about time you 'fessed up about your fairer—and supposedly—weaker sex. Men don't know the rules anymore, and it isn't until they realize that the women don't know, either, that they can ever begin to win."

Laura leaned back. "What's this thing about winning or losing? Men equate everything they do to those words. Can't more than one person win, and aren't there several ways to do so?"

Chuckling, David gave up. "You're right, I'm sure. And I'm certainly not going to argue the point with a pro debater. But I bet I could beat you in a wrestling contest," he declared with a leer.

She giggled, leaning her head on his shoulder and cuddling closer, knowing just what kind of an ending that would lead to. "It's a prime example of what I've been talking about. I contend that if I lose your wrestling contest, I win."

"Women's logic escapes me, but whatever you say is usually right on target." He sighed, pretending defeat as he stood with her tightly clasped in his arms. "Ready to prove your point?"

She wrapped her arms around his neck and kissed the strong, tanned column of his throat. "Ready."

KATHERINE AND CONSUELA finished wiping the kitchen counters, erasing the last traces of dinner for six in the older woman's large, old-fashioned kitchen. It was their night to clean, each two members of the family trading off this duty and almost every other chore to be done in the household.

Consuela's family was wonderful. They were rowdy and loving and full of fun, but they worked hard to ensure that each of them got ahead in a world that was filled with enough stumbling blocks to overwhelm a lone individual.

Katherine had lived with Consuela for almost two weeks now, and as soon as she received her next paycheck she'd be renting an apartment of her own. Last week she had returned Clay's car, parking it in front of the office with a short thank-you note attached.

Leaning her hip against the counter, she glanced around the slightly shabby room. "I'm going to miss it here," she mused aloud.

Consuela rinsed her washrag. "Then don't go. Stay."

Katherine smiled, but it didn't erase the sadness in her eyes. "I can't. It's time to stand on my own two feet." She glanced around again, taking in the often-scrubbed wallpaper that was as outdated as the paper at her brother's home. "But I'll still miss it."

Consuela folded the cloth neatly, then draped it over the faucet. "How is the job working out? Is that framerman training you properly?"

"Not as well as you were," Katherine teased, showing some of her old spirit. "But he's trying. And I'm learning."

"Hmph," Consuela answered. "You've got lots of smarts and they shouldn't go for the wrong things, young lady. You need that schooling."

Katherine pulled away from the counter and rinsed her own cloth. "I know. And I'll do it this September at the business school. By then I'll have enough money and be in my job long enough to prove I'm a good risk for another loan." She refused to think of her earrings. She had given them to Clay in love, and despite everything, they were where they belonged.

"Have you contacted Clay yet?" Consuela knew the answer to this, but it was the one question she asked at least three times a week.

"Not yet."

"When?" The older woman's sharp eyes took in the shadows under Katherine's eyes, the drawn, unhappy look that had been there since she'd arrived almost two weeks ago.

"Soon," she promised wearily. "I put a letter in the mail to him today."

"He's not himself anymore," Consuela muttered as she placed a full pot of water on the stove and turned on the burner. "I've never seen him like this. I don't like it."

"Is he angry?"

"No. He's just not the same. Like someone took all the stuffing out of him and threw it around the room. He sees it, but he's not interested enough to stuff it back into his shirt."

"Like a scarecrow?"

Her dark eyes pinned the younger woman. "Like a man who just lost the woman he loves. Nothing else matters except her."

Katherine turned and opened the refrigerator. Taking out a dozen eggs, she handed them to Consuela. "You're wrong. He made it more than plain that he wasn't in love. In fact, the last thing he needs is me."

Consuela took the eggs and began placing them in the pan. Lunch for six tomorrow would be egg salad. "Don't go by how he acts. He's always been that way. The boy was raised under rotten circumstances and he's grown his own armor around him. You were the first one he let in."

She thought of her own life and how hard it had been and felt herself bristling. "He lied to me about his engagement to Magda! Purposely! Besides, half of us have rotten circumstances. Why were his any different?"

"Well," Consuela sighed, reaching in the cupboard for two wineglasses and pouring a generous amount of ruby-red Mogan-David wine in both of them. She handed one to Katherine, then sat at the Formica-topped table. "His mother and father had big problems. Still do. But when he was young and impressionable, they fought and bickered over everything, especially him. His mother used him as a weapon against his father. Then she used him as a weapon against her own feelings. She would give him gifts, then swear that she had to pay for it out of private funds because his father kept her penniless. She'd tell him he just wasn't worth her poor saved-together money. Then she'd tell his father that he was worthless as a man, and if it wasn't for her, he wouldn't even have his son's love."

"Was it true?" Katherine's voice was almost a whisper.

"No, but I think he believed it anyway. And most of the time, Clay was in the middle, loving both of them, especially his mother, until she finally turned on him and tore him to shreds with her belittling tongue. Nowadays they call it emotional child abuse, but in those days parents were gods."

Katherine leaned back, imagining Clay as a boy. It went a long way toward explaining his tendency to be a loner, not trusting anyone, especially a woman. No one except Laura and Consuela. "How do you know this is true?"

The older woman's face turned to stone. "Because I was their maid for over ten years. I saw it all. Some of it couldn't even bear repeating, it was so awful. I watched him retreat until there was no one to retreat from anymore."

Katherine was stunned. Her mind churned over the story, her imagination recreating scenes she was sure had taken place. "But...one woman, even his mother, couldn't have changed his life that drastically," she finally objected.

"It helped. From that point on it seemed that the women he chose had the same outlook as his mother had. Right up to Magda. They were all people who were selfish with their emotions, going through the actions of caring, but only when it suited them or when they needed something." Her voice was filled with derision. "And not having any experience of what a real family was like or what more than one or two friends were for, didn't help."

"I see." She slowly twirled her untouched glass. But it still didn't explain a lot of things.

Consuela gazed at her for a long silent moment. "None of us knows another person completely, Katherine, but I'd venture a guess that Clay just really didn't know how to deal with you. You see, he cared too much to know how to act and that scared him even more. When it comes to relationships, he's always been a cautious man." She stood and put her empty wineglass in the sink. "And that's my ration of philosophy for the night. It's time for my favorite program." She walked toward the living room where her family had gathered after dinner, her soft slippers scuffing against the linoleum floor. High-heeled shoes and office dresses were discarded the moment she walked into the house.

"Consuela?"

She halted at the doorway, looking over her shoulder in silent inquiry.

"How did you go from being a maid to being a head secretary?"

"Clay sent me to secretarial school the year he graduated." She grinned. "He knew it was what I wanted to do—just like you. I borrowed the money from him and by the time he opened his business, I was trained, experienced and ready to take on the job."

Katherine should have known. "For a man who hates love, he sure has enough people loving him," she muttered dourly.

Consuela laughed as she left the room, tossing one more remark over her shoulder. "*Niña*, nobody ever has enough people loving them!"

CLAY'S MUSCLES TENSED as he reached toward a particular letter in the pile of mail he'd been sorting through. He knew that handwriting well. He darted a glance toward Consuela who was sitting at the phone taking down a message, then he slipped the envelope into his coat pocket and walked into his office, shutting the door.

Fear and anticipation warred inside him. Was she ready to see him again? Was she telling him that he was no good? He was certain the answers were inside the sealed envelope, but he wasn't quite brave enough to open it and find out.

He glanced at the calendar on his desk. It was two weeks and three days since he'd seen Katherine last. A lifetime. A long, lonely, boring, depressing lifetime.

Every night he turned toward her side of the bed, his arms reaching out for her, only to find emptiness. Every evening he waited for the sound of her delight at certain music or a passage in a book that would please her enough to share it with him, only to find the room void of warmth. Every ring of the phone was a jump-start for his heart, and depression followed quickly to envelop him when he didn't hear her voice on the line.

Her earrings had become his talisman.

He'd had plenty of time to think. He'd been wrong so many times in his relationships, but now he knew why. No one ever received something without giving something in return. Money for goods. Love for love.

He'd spent his lifetime slowly shriveling up emotionally. The picture of his behavior until now wasn't pretty, and if Katherine hadn't come along to show him what he'd been missing, he doubted that he ever would have found the door to happiness.

The funny thing now was that he finally had the key, only there was no one on the other side of the door. Katherine was gone and he hadn't been able to find her.

Two swift raps on the door made him jump guiltily. Consuela didn't wait for his invitation, but peered around the door, her eyes bright. "Coffee and cookies?" she asked.

He looked at her warily. "What kind?"

Her face looked like a blank piece of wrinkled paper. "Wedding cookies."

"Forget it, unless you can deliver the bride."

"All in good time, Mr. Reynolds."

His eyes narrowed. He stared at her a silent moment before he asked the question to which he already knew the answer. He'd been so steeped in his own misery he'd overlooked the obvious. "You know where she is, don't you?"

"Yes."

"But you won't tell me."

"No."

"Why in hell not? Why does everyone protect her from me as if I'd eat her for breakfast?" His frustration was apparent in every movement of his body.

"Because you already had one try and you almost did."

Harsh words from the woman who knew him best. He sighed, leaning back in his chair and running a hand through his hair. "Go away, Consuela. Leave me alone."

Her head disappeared and the door closed softly. After several minutes he finally reached into his coat pocket and withdrew the letter, setting it on his desk and staring at it.

Another five minutes passed before he found the nerve to read it. With a silver letter opener, he slit the top, careful to not rip the folded papers inside. The handwriting was soft, feminine, flowing. Just like her. He forced his eyes to focus on the words, while his mind wanted to wander down memory lane and revisit the loving scenes the scent of her paper aroused.

Dear Clay,
The enclosed bills were charged on your account when you told me to buy whatever mistresses were supposed to buy. Now that I no longer hold that position, I'm not sure what to do with the clothing. Please send instructions via Laura. May I

suggest that next time you put a limit on your accounts? You could pay for years on the damage one person could do in a day.

I'm putting my life back together now and things are looking up. Please don't try to find me anymore, I don't think it would do either of us any good to rehash the past only to reach the same conclusion again. We'd both walk away with a headache and probably say things that are better left unsaid.

I wish you all the luck in the world.

Always,

Her name was a curlicued scrawl that flipped his heart over.

"Consuela," he barked into the intercom. "Could you come in here, please? And bring me all the cookies you have left."

"Right away, boss." When she appeared at the door, he was openly grinning.

"I want you to locate a Montclair Castle or family or whatever you can find. It's in France." He grabbed a piece of paper and scribbled something on it, then held it out to her. "This is a picture of the crest. It might help."

"But . . . how?"

"Call a travel service that specializes in Europe. Call the library. Call France!"

Her grin could have split the world apart. "Right, boss."

Leaning back, he stared out the window. If anyone could get the information, Consuela could. He'd find Katherine's dream, and then he'd tell Katherine. . . .

After he'd drafted a reply to Katherine's letter, he left the office and played out the rest of his hunch. If Consuela knew where Katherine was, his bet was that she had found Katherine a job. And the one job that came to mind was in the office of the very people she had helped Beau sell the building to.

Later that afternoon he parked across the street from the building and waited. His nerves jumped each time the door opened. Then she appeared, her red hair brushed sedately back, a black grosgrain ribbon holding it in place. Her navy-blue dress clung to her curves without being obvious, and tall high heels that he had begun to think of as her trademark slimmed her already perfectly shaped legs. He couldn't take in enough of her.

She joked with one of the other girls who walked out, but there was still an aura of sadness about her. He wanted to see her happy again.

Just as he was about to step from the car and confront her, another car pulled up and she slipped in. Anger rushed through his veins as he recognized the man behind the wheel. His best friend. David.

David's car moved away soon and disappeared down the street. Clay was slow. It took him almost a minute to realize he had to follow in order to find out where she was living. And after he'd gotten that information he'd attack David.

It wasn't until they reached Consuela's street that the truth hit him. Everybody that mattered to him was in on this conspiracy to keep him from Katherine. Consuela, David, Laura. They all thought he would hurt the woman he loved. He'd never felt so alone in all his life.

That deep sense of loneliness drifted over him like a heavy blanket. Katherine wasn't being coy when she had said she didn't want to see him. She had truly cut him out of her life.

He pulled the car into a driveway and turned around, heading for home. There was no sense in confronting Katherine. Or David.

He'd lost.

CONSUELA GAVE KATHERINE the letter as two of her girls were preparing dinner. "This is for you, *niña*," she said, holding out the envelope.

Katherine glanced at her friend, coming out of her reverie. "Me? From who?"

"Whom. Clay."

She still didn't reach for it. Her heart beat faster at the sound of his name. "You told him?"

"Only that I knew where you were."

"What did he say?"

Consuela dropped the envelope into her lap. "He wrote this letter while he ate an entire plate of wedding cookies." Her tone was smug.

"What does it say?" She stared at the white envelope in her lap as if it were going to bite. "Is he still angry?"

"Read it," Consuela ordered softly as she walked out of the small living room. "I need to change."

Katherine's hands shook as she lifted the envelope flap and plucked out the folded white sheet with Clay's company name at the top. She scanned the contents first, then read it from the top—word for word.

Dearest Katherine,
Missing you is now a habit I can't shake. Your scent and presence are all around me, filling my

thoughts with visions of you. And instead of hating it, I find myself loving the hurt it gives me just to remember the times we had together. It's far better than feeling empty.

I stare at your earrings every hour, remembering the first time I met you. They capture the light in your eyes and remind me of the sparkle of your smile.

I was wrong. You weren't mine. You were never mine. I was yours.

Name your terms and come back to me.

Tears spilled down Katherine's cheeks even as she chuckled. The first two paragraphs were so beautiful, so unlike the Clay she had come to know, but the last line was a reminder of how much he still had to learn about personal relationships.

Damn the man! He still wouldn't admit that he loved her! Once, and in the throes of passion wasn't enough. She needed more. And so did he. The phone rang and she answered it, Clay's letter still clutched in her hand.

"Katherine? Laura. Clay left a card in my mailbox." Her breath stopped. "What did it say?"

"Thanks for being such a wonderful friend to Katherine. No one on earth deserves your care more."

"How right he is," she stated between gritted teeth. If sympathy was what he was after, it wasn't going to work on her. "Next time you see him, thank him for me."

"Katherine, don't you think you could just see him once? He's so . . ."

"Broken-hearted? Sad? Depressed?" she asked sarcastically.

"All of the above."

"Like hell he is!" Her anger finally got the better of her. "He's maneuvering all of us around like he's playing chess! Damn that man! It's working and I resent it!"

"But Clay *is* depressed and lonely!" Laura defended. "And he *does* love you!"

"Only until he has me in his hip pocket again. Then he thinks he can go blithely off to fight dragons, making sure that I'm tucked safe and secure in the castle tower."

Laura's laugh tinkled over the wires. "I think he already knows that won't work," she corrected. "Right now he's looking for options. From you."

"I'll give him options," she threatened. How dare he manipulate the people who love him like this! "I'll give him more choices than he knows what to do with!"

"Go to it, lady," Laura cheered. "But see him. Okay?"

"Okay," she promised. "But he might wish he never saw me!"

"Katherine, the man has learned more lessons in a month than most learn in a lifetime. Keep that in mind when you see him, won't you?"

"I'll give him a test to see how much he's grown," she returned. "And if he passes, I'll give him a star, but I'm still reserving the right to walk out."

"I'm praying he passes."

When Katherine hung up the phone, her mind was buzzing with alternatives that she checked and discarded. Then she smiled. One course of action would really knock him off base, which was exactly as it should be.

With hands that were suddenly calm, she dialed Clay's home number and waited for the answering device to click on. It did.

"Clay?" she said slowly, softly. "This is Katherine and I'd like to talk to you. Consuela knows where I am." She hesitated a moment for effect. Then with a voice that sounded as if it would break, she said, "I'll be waiting," and hung up.

Her emerald eyes gleamed. If Clay had declared war she couldn't be more ready. Only this time, if she played her cards right, they were both going to win—but not before Mr. Reynolds learned a lesson about the dangers of becoming a puppeteer. No one was going to pull Katherine O'Malley's strings unless she *allowed* them to!

12

CLAY PULLED INTO his driveway. It was still hard to believe that the woman he'd thought of as his substitute mother had been so afraid of his actions that she'd hidden Katherine from him. And his best friends! David and Laura both knew how Clay felt about her. How could they work so hard to keep Clay from the woman he loved?

He flipped the switch to activate the garage door opener, but he remained in the driveway. His hands returned to grip the steering wheel as if he were hanging on for dear life. The lump in his throat wouldn't disappear, but slowly anger welled up inside him, filling him and erasing the hurt.

Finally letting go of the wheel, he curled his hands into fists and hit the Porsche's wheel. Damn! He was sick and tired of being confused! But finally now, he wasn't anymore. Not since the morning he'd woken up to find Katherine gone.

Taking a deep breath, he forced himself to relax. He straightened his fingers and rested his hands on his pant legs. Then he reached inside his pocket, pulling out the small bag that held Katherine's earrings. He stared at them, feeling their weight in his hands. They were so small, but so very precious. Oh, not just because they were jewels, but because they were one of the first things about Katherine that had caught his eye. And she had given them to him in love. He was as sure of that as he was that they were created in the same name. His hand tightened.

It was time to act.

He put the car in reverse. Leaving his garage door opened, he sped down the quiet residential street and back toward the highway.

He was tired of being the emotional victim. Ever since he could remember he'd kept his business life and personal life separate. Compartmentalized. While his business flourished, his personal relationships never got off the ground. He'd allowed them to drift along rather than ending them himself. When he'd had to tell Magda that their engagement was over, it had almost hit him as hard as it had her. Had that been when he started to resent Katherine's emotional hold on him? He thought so. But try as he might, he hadn't been able to withdraw from her completely. She was in his blood. She belonged with him. For always!

He maneuvered the car down Consuela's street and pulled up to the curb. It was about time he took command of his personal life the same way he had his business.

His knock was loud and firm. His expression was bland, hiding the determination that flowed through him. His hands were steady. His eyes were clear with purpose. He knew what he wanted and he was going after it.

KATHERINE SHOOED Consuela back to the couch and her family's favorite situation comedy, before opening the door. Her jaw dropped and her heartbeat quickened when she saw Clay.

He took up all the room in the doorway. His hands were clenched into fists at his sides. His eyes were glazed

with either anger or pain, she wasn't sure which. He was
staring at her. It was the only reassuring thing about
him: he wanted her and it came through in silent language.

"Are you ready?"

She looked at him, still confused. "Ready for what?"

"For this," he said and he reached out to draw her
against him. "I've been patient long enough," he muttered before his lips possessed hers in a kiss that made
her head spin. He pressed her to him, and she reveled
in the luscious feelings only he was capable of arous-
ing. His tongue ravished her mouth, then softened to a
most intimate caress. With his hands he rubbed her
back as if impressing her softer image upon his own
hard body.

She wrapped her arms around his neck and held on,
her mind swirling. But there was something niggling in
the back of her mind. . . .

She pushed against his shoulders and he allowed her
to pull away. Just a little. "Just what do you think you're
doing?" she asked breathlessly, trying to stir up the anger she knew she was supposed to feel. "I just asked you
to call, not to take me over as if I was a piece of land for
development."

He frowned. "What are you talking about."

"My call? Isn't that what this is all about?"

"When did you call?"

Her eyes widened. "You didn't know?"

He shook his head. "But I do now. And it just con-
firms my feelings. You're coming with me."

"Where? Why?"

Clay glared down at her. "I'm taking you with me so
we can have a long talk."

He was acting unyielding, but two could play at that game. She crossed her arms, her stance pure defiance. "I'm not going anywhere with you, Clay Reynolds."

"Yes, you are." His mouth clamped shut and he once more reached for her, picking her up in his arms as if she were the bride he was carrying over a threshold. With determination etching his features, he stalked down the front walkway. His grip was firm, holding her tightly but still being careful not to hurt her, even as she struggled.

"Put me down!" she screamed, pounding on his shoulder and back.

"What's going on?" Consuela's voice filtered through their anger, succeeding in stopping Clay.

He turned, meeting the eyes of the woman he'd known since childhood. "I'm taking Katherine for a long conversation." Her face, without the makeup she usually wore, was older and more tired. Her eyes locked with his, definite questions lurking there. Katherine didn't move as she watched with fascination the silent byplay between them.

Consuela's brows met over the bridge of her nose. "You're sure?"

"Positive." He grinned. "She'll call you in the morning and let you know all the gory details."

Consuela nodded, apparently convinced of the rightness of the thing. "Okay. I'll call her boss and tell him she's got an appointment."

Clay's eyes narrowed. "A long one. She may not be back."

Without realizing she was doing it, Katherine had wound her arms around Clay's neck. Suddenly she tightened her hands. "That's my decision, Clay Reynolds! Not yours."

He looked back at Consuela. "It's negotiable."

Consuela chuckled. "Isn't everything?"

With that Clay turned toward his car once more and didn't stop until Katherine was belted into the passenger seat. She sat quietly, suddenly docile, and waited for him to explain his bizarre actions. He had come to get her, not knowing she had called. He wanted her with him badly enough to take the chance he wouldn't be received well.

He started up the engine and drove quickly but surely out of the neighborhood.

"Well?" she said when she couldn't contain herself any longer. "Is there an apology in this?"

"No."

"Then let me out."

"Not until you hear what I have to say."

"Anytime soon?"

"In an hour." His mouth was grim, and she decided to go along with whatever he had in store. He had never hurt her, and she was positive he wasn't going to start now. Even Consuela trusted him. Katherine had confidence he'd do no more than break her heart.

She recognized the road. They were on their way back to Canyon Lake. Was he going to take her out in the middle of the lake until this "talk" was over? A delicious feeling flowed through her. It should have been fear, but she was honest enough to admit that it was excitement. She wasn't excited enough, however, to lose sight of the fact that he was only angry with her for leaving. There was no reason to get her hopes up. Clay would always be Clay: a man who'd had too many bad experiences with women to allow her to be part of the very essence of his life. And she would settle for no more than that.

The lake house was dark. Clay stopped the car in front of the door and turned to face her. "Ready?"

"You keep asking that," she said, frowning. "Yet you won't tell me what I'm supposed to be ready for."

He sighed. "Come on in. We can't talk here."

"Why not?"

"Because it's too cramped." He stepped out and walked around, opening her door for her. When she accepted his hand Katherine knew she'd follow him anywhere. She'd forget being contrary just because she didn't like his high-handed attitude; she wanted to hear what he had to say.

The house was as beautiful inside as she had imagined it would be. It might have been molded after a log cabin, but that was the only similarity between this house and any other cabin Katherine had seen. There were cathedral ceilings in every room, the white plaster contrasting with dark-stained pine logs. The furniture was contemporary instead of country as she would have expected. A loose-cushioned, white "playpen" couch sat in front of the rock fireplace that took up an entire wall. The other wall was glass that curved up to the ceiling, like a greenhouse, and the view of the lake was spectacular. A full moon bounced off the water and created diamond drops moving across the cove to the outer lake.

"Drink?" Clay asked, moving to the open kitchen in the corner.

"Please." She was going to need a little fortification. "Wine?"

"Yes." She walked to the window, stepping around the plants that grew so profusely inside. Her back was to the room. Suddenly she could feel herself trembling from deep inside, the tremors working their way out through shaky hands and knees. But she refused to let him see. . . .

"Beautiful view, isn't it?" Clay said as he handed her the glass. "It always calms me."

"And are you calm now?" she asked before sipping on the cool liquid.

"No. When you're around, I'm anything but." His voice had lowered, turning intimate and sexy. It reminded her of when he made love and whispered endearments in her ear. Her nerves tensed even more.

"Then I suggest we get this talk over with, so we can both go about our business. Separately." Was that her talking? She sounded so cool, so collected. Thank goodness!

He took a step away from her, retreating, and her heart sank. "Katherine, I love you."

"You said that," she replied, unable to keep the bitterness out of her voice. "Once, I believe. You just forgot to put the finish on it."

Piercing brown eyes dared her to look at him. She refused. "What's the finish?"

"The finish was something along the lines of loving me enough to sleep with me, but not enough to marry. Or to tell the truth to, or to live with forever. Or to trust."

"I just wanted to pick the time we came together and make up my own mind. Not be forced into it."

She finally turned, confronting him. Her eyes were blazing with anger and hurt, but she didn't care. "So I made the decision for you, Clay. I left so you wouldn't be put in a position of refusing me."

"Were you asking me to marry you?"

His matter-of-fact tone drove her temper to the brink. "What the hell do you think I was doing? Of course I was!"

"Then I accept," he stated calmly, and her mouth dropped open.

She snapped it shut. "This is no time for jokes. Say what you have to say and let's get this over with."

"I just did."

Katherine walked into the living room and placed the glass on a table. When she turned, Clay was standing where she had left him, his brown eyes sending her messages she couldn't begin to fathom. His sandy colored hair glinted in the overhead light and her fingers itched to run through the thick mass. But he was too far away....

Her pulse was erratic, her heart threatening to jump out of her body. "Let me get this straight. You're accepting my proposal of marriage, which I never formally issued, because you've finally decided all on your own that this is the time and place to marry."

"I love you and I want to marry you."

"Then why didn't you ask me before I left?"

"Because I was fighting my feelings for you. You came into my life and, like a whirlwind, you turned everything topsy-turvy. I wasn't thinking straight so I relied on my old method and tried not to make any decisions at all." His voice vibrated through her soul, then filled her mind.

"Then why are you all the way across the room?" she whispered.

"Because if I come any closer to you, I'm going to drag you in there—" he nodded toward a partially closed door "—and make love to you until neither of us can move. Then we'd never get our feelings straightened out."

She nodded as if she understood, when all she wanted him to do was exactly that. "Fire away."

He looked startled. "At what?"

"Your feelings. I've always worn mine on my sleeve, Mr. Reynolds. You're the mystery here. For instance, why wouldn't you tell me about Magda? Didn't you know how guilty I felt every time I lusted after another woman's man?" That thought brought back her anger. Thankfully. Anything was better than melting into a puddle at his feet!

"Because I resented the fact that you had such a tight hold over my heart. I used Magda as a weapon against you, only it didn't work." He looked so handsome. So contrite. So damned miserable. Her heart began to heal and he hadn't said more than a few words!

His eyes roamed her face hungrily. "I love you." His voice soothed her like dark, warm molasses. "I love you so much I ache with it."

"I thought you didn't believe in love." Her voice was shaking as much as her knees were.

"I was wrong. I was wrong about a lot of things."

"But now you've learned everything."

He shook his head, his eyes not leaving her face. "The only thing I've learned is that I don't know much about life and love. You've taught me that, Katherine."

Her eyes narrowed. Could this be some kind of trick? Clay had never been humble. "I'm happy for you."

"I've missed you. I can't sleep without you next to me. Everywhere I turn, your ghost is there, reminding me what a fool I was."

He took a step closer and, perversely, she wished he would retreat. She couldn't breathe. "We'd never make

it. I don't have the education you do. I'm not that good
with your clients, your friends. I'd embarrass you."

He took another step closer, determination filling his
movements. "You can get an education, if that's what
you want. Although you're smart in a sense most people never are. You have knowledge of people and their
thoughts and emotions. You seem to have a sixth sense
about it, and that can't be learned. You're great with my
clients, open and honest. Not a 'yes' woman who would
bore the hell out of them. My friends all adore you.
Dave drives you to work. Consuela thinks you're one
of her baby chicks. Laura considers you her best friend.
Even Drake thinks you're the best thing in my life."

He took another step. "Embarrass me?" He shrugged.
"Probably. But it only means that I'm a stuffed shirt on
occasion and you're good for me. You shake me up,
bring sunshine into my life, make me think of things I
would never have thought of without you. You fill me
with love and laughter and feelings that grant me
peace."

"I'm a paragon of virtue," she muttered, wishing the
couch cushion wasn't pressing against her thighs. The
only direction to go was down. She sat. "But I think
you've got the terms mixed up. I fill you with lust and
possessiveness. I can handle the first one, but I'm not a
thing to be owned, Clay."

His brown eyes turned heavy with sadness. "I know
that now. Don't you think I knew how badly I was
treating you? But I couldn't stop. I couldn't trust. I was
waiting for you to prove me wrong—to prove that you
wanted all the things I could give you instead of me, the
person. Good and bad."

"You never gave me a chance to prove what I
wanted," she said softly, the sadness in her eyes match-

ing his. "I have nothing to offer you, Clay. No money or family or connections or education. So I gave you the only thing I owned. Me. It was my gift to you."

"And a pair of earrings with a history of love. Something you treasured beyond yourself. They've become my talisman these past few weeks. The only hope I had of your love."

"You knew?"

He nodded. "You wouldn't have parted with them if love—deep love—wasn't involved. I was just too stubborn and hardheaded to know it at the time."

"Smart man." Her voice was low, a lump in her throat causing her to swallow hard.

There was no happiness in his smile. "No. I was stupid. With the evidence in my hand, I still refused to see it." He closed his eyes. When he opened them again, she saw the vulnerability that he'd never allowed her to see before. "There's nothing I can do to change the past, Katherine. But I can change the future if you let me. We can. Together. Do you trust me enough to take my word for it?"

Her slow smile could have lit the entire room. "I think we could give it a try."

He pulled his gaze away from her just long enough to find the piece of paper he was looking for in his breast pocket. "With every contract offer, there's a counteroffer." He watched her beautiful face become lined with puzzlement. "This is my counteroffer."

Reluctantly she accepted the piece of paper, her heart dropping into the pit of her stomach. She unfolded it slowly. "It's a marriage license," she finally managed, her throat almost closed with knowledge.

"For us."

Katherine stared at it, tears in her eyes. She nodded her head and Clay pulled her into his arms. "Is that a yes or a no?" he asked, his mouth nuzzling the side of her neck. "Say something, dammit, before I go out of my mind!"

"Yes," she whispered. "Yes," she repeated in a stronger voice. "Yes!" she shouted, throwing her arms around his neck as if she'd never let go. Her buoyant spirits were out of control.

His kiss held the promise of everything bright and new and open and true. When she pulled away, she rested her head on his chest and heard the answer to her own quickened heartbeat in his.

"Do we sign any other kind of contract?" she whispered.

"To *hell* with contracts! This is a marriage—not a merger!"

Her fingertips slid over his well-formed lips, a small spritely smile on hers. "You win, Clay," she said with a sigh.

"Thank God, you little leprechaun." His voice was rough with feeling. "A friend of mine, a judge, has got the morning of the twenty-eighth set aside for our wedding."

"Suddenly you're making decisions left and right," she murmured, her hand busy with the buttons on his shirt.

"You're damn right," he muttered against her soft nape. "If you'd answered any other way, I was going to hold you here as my prisoner until you agreed."

"Such a novel idea," she purred.

"I have a better one. After the wedding we're flying to France for our honeymoon. We can do what your parents always wanted to do and trace the original owners of your jewelry."

"How?"

"Consuela found the Montclair Castle. It's a luxury resort now, and I've made a reservation for a two weeks' stay, starting the day after tomorrow and ending the first week in July."

"You're really taking time off work?"

"With Consuela keeping tabs on business, no one will miss me."

"At least for a while," Katherine said, her fingers teasing his neck.

"And you're taking back those earrings. I want you wearing them every time I make love to you. I saw them on you the first day I met you and I want to see them on you when I die."

Then Clay Settles Reynolds kissed Katherine Maureen O'Malley, sealing with his lips what had already been engraved upon his heart.

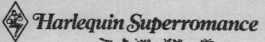

Harlequin Superromance

**Here are the longer, more involving stories you
have been waiting for... Superromance.**

Modern, believable novels of love, full of the complex
joys and heartaches of real people.

Intriguing conflicts based on today's constantly
changing life-styles.

Four new titles every month.
Available wherever paperbacks are sold.

ABANDON YOURSELF TO

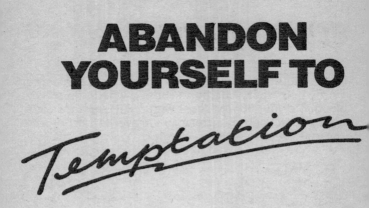

Temptation

TEMPTATION WILL BE EVEN HARDER TO RESIST...

In September, Temptation is presenting a sophisticated new face to the world. A fresh look that truly brings Harlequin's most intimate romances into focus.

What's more, all-time favorite authors Barbara Delinsky, Rita Clay Estrada, Jayne Ann Krentz and Vicki Lewis Thompson will join forces to help us celebrate. The result? A very special quartet of Temptations...

- **Four striking covers**
- **Four stellar authors**
- **Four sensual love stories**
- **Four spellbinding jewels**
- **THE MONTCLAIR EMERALDS...** you'll be dazzled!

The Montclair Emeralds . . . a priceless symbol of enduring love from a French nobleman to his lady. . . The jewels have traveled from seventeenth-century France, through time and circumstance, to four far-flung corners of twentieth-century America. To this day, they are still working their magic—a legacy of undying passion to the lovers who possess them. . . .

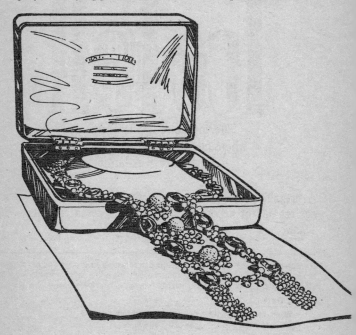